The
Hardy Boys™
Handbook

Seven Stories
of Survival

The Hardy Boys™ Handbook

Seven Stories of Survival

by Franklin W. Dixon
In collaboration with survival instructor
Sheila Link
Illustrated by Leslie Morrill

WANDERER BOOKS

Published by
SIMON & SCHUSTER, NEW YORK

Copyright © 1980 by Stratemeyer Syndicate
All rights reserved
including the right of reproduction
in whole or in part in any form
Published by Wanderer Books
A Simon & Schuster Division of
Gulf & Western Corporation
Simon & Schuster Building
1230 Avenue of the Americas
New York, New York 10020

Manufactured in the United States of America
10 9 8 7 6 5 4 3 2 1

Wanderer and colophon are trademarks
of Simon & Schuster

Library of Congress Cataloging in Publication Data

Dixon, Franklin W.
The Hardy boys handbook.

CONTENTS: Survival kits.—Winter wilderness.—
Lonely ordeal. [etc.]
1.   Children's stories, American.
[1.   Survival—Fiction] I.   Link, Sheila,
joint author.   II.   Title.
PZ7.D644Har   [Fic]   79-27885

ISBN 0–671–95705–8
ISBN 0–671–95602–7 pbk.

Contents

Each of the seven stories of survival were drawn from an actual experience. The survival equipment and methods recommended have been field-tested by the consultant.

1.
Frank and Joe Pack Survival Kits

"I'm sure glad Dad talked us into taking that course in survival," Frank said as he expertly eased the car into the garage and turned off the ignition.

"So am I," Joe agreed, reaching over into the back seat. He handed several parcels to Frank, then gathered up the rest. "Even though we learned a lot in scouting," Joe continued, "Professor Henry discussed things I never heard about."

"How true!" Frank held the door open and the Hardy boys entered the house. "Especially that business about the basic priorities of life—remember?"

"You mean what the professor called the Rule of Three?" Joe nodded. "Sure never knew that we can live for three minutes without air, three days without water, and for three *weeks* without food."

Frank winked at his younger brother teasingly. "You always believed that cheeseburgers and chocolate malts were the basic necessities of life!"

Joe grinned sheepishly, then answered, "Well, I *did* think of food as being more important than shelter—but now I know better."

"That was fascinating, wasn't it?" Frank responded serious-ly. "Learning how vital it is to provide shelter in order to keep your body temperature as near normal as possible." He placed his armful of packages on the table.

"Fascinating, but frightening, too," Joe answered, "to think how swiftly our minds are affected when our temperature goes much higher or lower than normal. And to realize that then we can't make wise decisions for ourselves, that we can become so dependent upon someone else. . . ." His voice trailed off.

"Right," Frank replied, "but thanks to Professor Henry, we now know what the real priorities of life are and, regardless of circumstances, how to provide for them." He hesitated. "And how important it is that we carry survival kits so we can take care of ourselves in any emergency."

Joe, hands on hips, nodded in agreement.

"Let's see now—have we got everything we need to put the survival kits together?" He faced Frank across the kitchen ta-ble. Carefully they scrutinized the jumble of assorted items spread in front of them. Some of the things were gathered from household supplies but the boys had bought most of the arti-cles that afternoon.

"It sure looks like it," Joe answered. "So let's get busy and start with the small pocket kits."

Frank grinned at his eager younger brother. "Why don't you read off what's on that list Professor Henry gave us and I'll put each item aside, one for you and one for me."

"Okay," said Joe, unfolding the list of survival kit contents. "The first thing is a container in which to carry everything."

Frank nodded as he placed two small zippered nylon belt packs, a dark green one for Joe and a blaze-orange one for himself, at one end of the table.

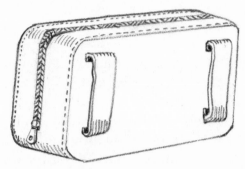

"Item two, a plastic lawn bag," Joe read as Frank opened a large new package, removed two folded bags, and laid one on top of each belt pack.

"Next, twenty feet of nylon parachute cord—wait, I'll have to help you with that," Joe said.

The boys measured two twenty-foot lengths of cord, which

they coiled neatly and put with the other articles. Joe picked up the lawn bag and cord, hefted them in his hand and said, "It's hard to believe *this* can make an adequate shelter!"

"Not if you stress the word *adequate,*" Frank responded, winking. "This is a *survival* kit we're putting together, not a camping outfit."

"That's right," Joe laughed. "I keep forgetting . . . Okay, what's next? A Metal Match and a chunk of steel wool."

"Got 'em," Frank said, and added, "This Metal Match is a great gadget." He held up the tiny rod of semisoft alloy. "It's so easy to strike a spark from it with a knife blade. But when Professor Henry recommended steel wool for tinder, he really surprised me."

"Me too," agreed Joe, "but he's right. You want something that'll catch fire even when it's wet, and no other material will do that. Hey! Are you sure our steel wool is fine enough?"

"Yes," Frank answered, holding up the box. Joe read the label aloud: VERY FINE TRIPLE-ZERO STEEL WOOL. He watched as Frank pulled two egg-sized wads from the thick pad and put them into two plastic sandwich bags along with two Metal Matches.

"Now what?" he asked, as Joe consulted the list.

"The candles," Joe replied.

Frank added two four-inch candles to the steel wool and Metal Matches, then closed the plastic bags tightly. "Heat and light," he said, and put them on the growing piles of survival items.

"Heavy-duty aluminum foil," Joe read, pointing to the un-opened box on the table. "Four or five feet."

Frank pulled off two generously measured five-foot lengths. "Give me a hand," he asked, "so we can fold them neatly."

The boys cleared the end of the table, then proceeded to fold the sheets lengthwise until they were only three inches wide. Next they folded them across, flattening each into a three-inch by four-inch pad.

"That's plenty," Frank said. "Not only for a fire reflector, but also for cooking or making a drinking cup."

"Funny you should mention *that*," grinned Joe, "for our next item is a Sierra Club cup." He pointed to the two squat,

wide-mouthed steel cups they'd bought that afternoon.

"Aluminum foil makes a perfectly usable cup or cooking pot in an emergency," Joe continued, "but those Sierra cups are a lot less fragile, not to mention being easier to use." Frank agreed as he placed the cups with the other things.

"Moving right along," Joe smiled, "we come to signal mirrors." Frank unwrapped a package marked ARMY-NAVY STORE and took out two three-inch by five-inch G.I. mirrors that had centered peepsights to assist in directing signals accurately.

"Right-o," he said, adding a mirror to each kit. "Now what?"

"The whistles," Joe replied.

Frank shook a pair of plastic whistles from a small bag. "Remember what Professor Henry said?" he asked. Then added, imitating the instructor's deep voice, "Don't ever use a metal whistle in subfreezing weather because—" here Frank held one to his outthrust lower lip, "you might get terribly *attached* to it!" Both boys laughed.*

"Next," Joe continued, "we come to wire saws."

"I think I'll leave these in the plastic envelopes," Frank said. "That seems the safest way to keep them." He held up the two flat packets, each containing a coiled eighteen-inch length of flexible, toothed wire with a ring at both ends. "I'd sure hate to cut up a cord of firewood with one of these!" he added.

"So would I," Joe concurred, "but Professor Henry said they'll do a good job in an emergency." He looked at the list. "Now let's see—oh, Band-Aids, bouillon packets, and Charms."

"Got 'em," Frank said, then asked, "Do you remember why the candy had to be Charms?"

---

*They had learned that metal would stick to the lips if the temperature were below freezing.

"Yes," Joe answered. "It doesn't *have* to be Charms but it should be a candy or sweet powdered drink made with glucose instead of sugar, so it'll give quick energy without being absorbed into the bloodstream or drawing body water into the stomach. Charms are recommended because they are easily available."

"Well, little brother, you really were paying attention in class, weren't you!"

Joe acknowledged Frank's compliment with a quick grin before he resumed reading from the list.

"Insect repellent, water purification tablets, and a single-edged razor blade," he said, as Frank placed a small plastic bottle of bug repellent and a tiny bottle of Potable Aqua tablets for purifying water with each stack of survival items. Before adding the razor blades, he taped a protective cardboard sheath over the sharp edges.

"Next we have a choice," Joe announced, "either a needle and thread or several safety pins—what'll you have?"

"I'll take some pins," Frank replied. "I'd do a terrible job of sewing, and anyway, this is for keeping clothes mended in an emergency, not for a fashion show!"

"Well, I don't like the idea of sewing any better than you do," Joe commented, "but I think a needle and thread are more practical."

While Frank slid four pins over the pointed end of another, snapped the holding pin shut, and placed them on his stack of articles, Joe wrapped two needles and a small card of various colored thread in a tiny square of foil for himself.

THE HARDY BOYS HANDBOOK

"Lip balm and a bandanna winds it up," Joe announced, "except for any personal additions."

"I think we should toss in some multivitamins," Frank advised. "What do you say?"

"That's a good idea," Joe retorted, "as long as we remember to replace them every few months—otherwise they'll be ineffective. I also think a few aspirin might come in handy."

The boys wrapped four multivitamin tablets in one small piece of aluminum foil and four aspirin tablets in another.

Each boy then carefully packed everything in his own seven-inch by five-inch by two-inch nylon belt pack. Frank placed his on the kitchen scale, then turned to Joe.

"Guess what it weighs?" he challenged. Joe hefted his filled kit in one hand, looked thoughtful for a moment then spoke with great assurance. "A pound and a quarter!"

"Wrong!" Frank said.

"Two pounds?"

"Nope—exactly three-quarters of a pound!"

Joe weighed his kit and found it the same. He turned to Frank. "There's no excuse for ever leaving these behind. We can carry them on our belts, or even in a pocket."

"That's the whole idea," Frank rejoined. "Remember what Professor Henry said? 'Keep pocket survival kits small and light enough so you won't mind carrying them.' "

"Yes," Joe nodded. "And he also said, 'The niftiest survival kit ever assembled is no good at all if it's back in camp or at home when you need it.' "

Frank smiled at Joe. "Okay, now let's put together kits for the car, the boat, and the snowmobiles."

Since it wasn't critical to keep these kits so small and light, the boys added aluminized Space Blankets, G.I. canteens, signal flares, and two cans of hearty soup to each kit. They packed them in sturdy plastic containers with lids that sealed tightly. Then Frank took a waterproof marking pen and printed FRANK AND JOE HARDY on top of each kit.

"Well, Joe, this was a good evening's work," he said as they began putting away the unused materials.

"I'm sure glad we got it all done," Joe replied. "But isn't it strange to spend so much time preparing something you hope you'll never use?"

"Better to have and not need," Frank stated, "than need and not have."

15

Contents of Personal Survival Kit

Pack into a small zippered nylon belt pouch:

1. Plastic lawn bag
2. 20 feet nylon parachute cord
3. Metal Match
4. Steel wool (.000)
5. Candle
6. Aluminum foil (5′ × 5′)
7. Signal mirror
8. Plastic whistle
9. Sierra Club cup
10. Wire saw
11. Band-Aids
12. Bouillon packets
13. Charms candy
14. Insect repellent
15. Lip balm
16. Water purification tablets
17. Single-edge razor blade (or knife)
18. Sewing kit (or assortment of safety pins)
19. Bandanna
20. Multivitamins
21. Aspirin

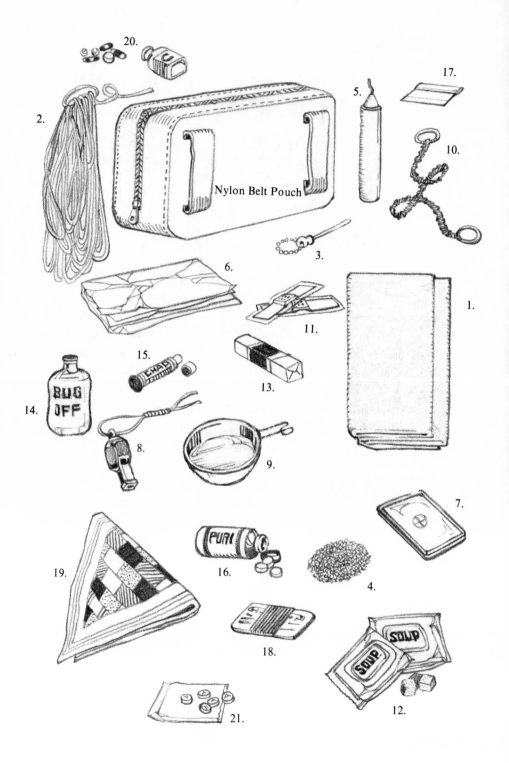

20.

2.

5.

17.

10.

Nylon Belt Pouch

3.

6.

11.

1.

15.

13.

14.

BUG OFF

8.

9.

7.

19.

PURI

16.

4.

18.

SOUP

SOUP

21.

12.

2.
Winter Wilderness

"Whooee!" cried Joe, as he glided to a stop beside Frank and leaned lightly on his ski poles. "What a neat hill!"

"I'll say," agreed Frank. "That nice downhill run felt great after such a long stretch of herringboning* up that slope."

"There's the trail." Joe pointed to a bright yellow marker at the edge of the trees ahead.

Frank, however, pulled the topo map† and compass out of his pocket. "Hold up a minute," he cautioned. "I want to check the direction and the distance."

The boys had been enticed to an unfamiliar section of New Hampshire's snow-covered mountains by a ski brochure that proclaimed, "This region of the White Mountains is a cross-country skier's paradise. Seventy-five miles of well-marked touring trails connect a network of inns and lodges. Enjoy top-notch skiing with the comfort of knowing there's a hot meal

---

*Herringbone. Walking uphill on skis with the skis at a forty-five-degree angle.

†Topographical Maps. Prepared by the U.S. Geological Survey; show elevation from sea level, type of vegetation, and contour of the terrain.

18

and a warm bed awaiting you in one of the cozy inns."

This was their third day. That morning the boys had left Rocky Ledge Lodge and were skiing to Fieldstone Inn, where they had reserved dinner and two bunks for the night.

"According to the map," Frank said as he returned it and the compass to his pocket, "we've still got about nine miles to Fieldstone Inn."

"That'll be a cinch," Joe commented, "especially if there are plenty of good, long downhill slopes. It's only one o'clock."

"Right," agreed Frank. "But, you know, it's getting colder." He looked up and added, "It's getting overcast, too. We'd better move along."

Setting their poles firmly, both boys pushed off, resuming the cross-country skier's smooth, mile-eating glide.

The section of trail they were on, Frank noted, did not seem to be heavily used. Maybe, he reasoned, there were no tracks because of frequent fresh snowfall. His vague feeling of concern gave way to the sheer pleasure of slipping silently through such a beautiful wilderness. Even though the sky was darkening, the glistening snow gave the woods a brightness that heightened the rugged beauty of the tall, snow-laden pines.

"Still think it's gotten colder?" Joe teased when they pulled up to catch their breath after climbing another uphill stretch. Exertion had heated both boys and they had opened their jackets to ventilate and keep their clothing safely and comfortably dry.

"We're warm now," admitted Frank, "but haven't you noticed that the weather is changing? There's even a stiff breeze building."

"Yes, I did notice it," Joe retorted, "because as soon as we stop I cool off quickly."

They stood for a moment more, then by mutual consent dug in and schussed* down a short hill, then into another dense forest of birch and pine trees.

When they entered the woods, their pace was slowed considerably as the trail twisted and turned through the heavy forest growth. Several hillside crossings required caution in order to avoid slipping precipitously down the steep slopes. Another obstacle in their progress was the increasing number of boulders, some requiring tricky maneuvering to get around them, while other, smaller rocks were dangerously hidden by the thick blanket of snow. Neither Frank nor Joe wanted to risk a broken ski tip, since that would mean a long, difficult walk to Fieldstone Inn for a replacement.

Suddenly a powerful, roaring wind hit the deeply engrossed skiers.

"Cripes!" Frank yelled as the swirling snow, some off the ground, some fresh-falling, enveloped the boys. "Where did that come from?"

"I don't know, but we'd better not stay here!" Joe yelled back. "I can't see very far—where's the trail?"

"I can't make out the trail or the marker either," Frank admitted. "We'll have to use the map and compass." He dug them out of his pocket. The wind, though, made it impossible

---

*Schuss. Skiing swiftly, without checking speed, downhill.

to hold the map. In addition, the storm had reduced the light so much it was hard to read the compass.

"We'd better hole up somewhere," Frank suggested, "and let this blow over. It's only three o'clock, so there's nothing to worry about."

"I noticed some big rock formations about a quarter mile back. That might be a good place for shelter," Joe said.

"Good idea," concurred Frank. "We could get lost trying to go ahead, but we can still see our tracks. Let's move!"

They turned around and carefully retraced their ski marks. Vision was becoming increasingly limited, so they were forced to estimate where Joe had seen the rocky area. Soon, though, Frank pointed off to his left. "Is that the place?"

Joe peered into the swirling snowflakes. "I really can't tell, but it's the sort of place I had noticed. Let's take a look."

Before leaving the trail, Frank tied his bright red survival-kit bandanna to a sturdy tree limb as a marker. Then the boys cautiously skied toward the towering boulders.

"There's a spot that's almost a cave," Frank said. "What do you think?"

"I think we'd better get these skis off and get ourselves settled," Joe responded as he bent down and disengaged his bindings.

Working quickly, they cleared snow off the ground under the shallow rock outcropping.

"If we get a good fire going right up against that back wall," Frank suggested, "it ought to warm the place nicely. Then we can move the fire to the edge and get inside."

"Good plan," Joe agreed, "but we'll have to block the wind from coming in on the left."

Frank began to gather firewood, looking for standing dead trees because their wood would be drier than anything lying on the snowy ground. For kindling he reached up underneath the big pines, and snapped off the slender little branches next to the trunk. Since they were sheltered from above, they were brittle and dry.

While Frank foraged for firewood, Joe opened his survival kit and removed the plastic lawn bag. He leaned his and Frank's skis and poles in a parallel row against the exposed left side of the tiny, clamshell-shaped cave. Then with his pocket knife he slit the bag down one side and across the bottom. Carefully he wove the plastic sheet between the skis and poles, creating a snug windbreak.

Just as he finished, he heard Frank's voice, very faint in the distance, calling his name.

"Hi, Frank!" he yelled. "Here I am!" No answer. Joe shouted Frank's name again, waited a moment, then called again. There was a response, but it sounded fainter than before.

"Hey Frank—over here!" Joe shouted again and again, but got no response. He grabbed the plastic whistle from his survival kit and blew it, waiting every few moments to listen for Frank's reply. After what seemed a very long time, he heard Frank's voice, still from a distance, but clearly. Joe put the whistle back and called, "Frank! Right here!"

"I'm coming," Frank called. "Keep on yelling—I still can't see you!"

Finally Frank arrived, his arms full of firewood. "Boy, I've never been so glad to see you," he grinned, giving Joe a light, affectionate punch on the shoulder. "That whistle really cuts through better than your voice did."

"Why did you go so far?" Joe demanded almost angrily, not wanting his brother to know how concerned he'd been.

"There was nothing close by except small stuff, and mostly pine," Frank explained. "I figured we'd want some big chunks of long-lasting hardwood." He looked at the plastic wall. "Say, Joe, that's a neat windbreak you rigged." He had dropped the firewood and stood watching as Joe began to lay a fire.

"We'll put our survival kits to the test now," Joe said, as he separated a bit of steel wool and placed some of the finest kindling nearby. Then, holding his pocketknife firmly in his right hand with the blade parallel to the ground, he drew a Metal Match sharply upward against the blade, throwing a spark into the steel wool.

The steel wool ignited instantly. Joe leaned some slender little pine twigs against the tiny blaze, then added a slightly heavier piece. It would not catch, though—it was frozen solid. Patiently he began all over again, with the same disheartening results. He had no way to foresee the absolute necessity of having a fire that night. But Joe knew that he and Frank would be cold and miserable without heat, so he kept working. On the third try he was successful. The flame caught and the blaze grew gradually as he slowly added more and heavier wood. When the fire was burning steadily he turned to Frank.

"We'll let this burn in here for just a while before moving it."

Joe looked closely at Frank, who was still standing and watching but showed no apparent interest.

"Hey, Frank, are you all right?" he asked.

"Sure, I'm fine," Frank answered. "I'm just cold—guess I got chilled." His voice trailed off as he began to shiver uncontrollably.

"Well, no wonder!" Joe replied. "Your jacket's open. The fire will be going strong in a couple of minutes," he added as he bent to add another chunk of wood, "and then we'll be snug and warm."

Joe scraped a firepit along the open edge of their improvised shelter. Then he dug into his belt pack for the folded sheet of aluminum foil.

"Give me a hand, old buddy," he spoke to Frank. "Don't just stand there. You'll feel warmer if you move around and— hey, why don't you zip up your jacket?"

"Yeah, okay," Frank mumbled indifferently. He continued to stay where he was, and did not follow Joe's suggestion to close the front of his coat.

Joe was busy making a frame of branches, which he covered with the unfolded aluminum foil. He propped up the improvised reflector sheet behind the firepit, facing into the shallow cave.

"How about that? That reflector will push the heat right back into the cave." He looked up at his brother for approval, and immediately jumped to his feet.

"Frank! What's wrong?" Joe grabbed Frank's arm, peered into his face, and said again, "Frank! What's the matter?"

"Nuthin' . . . nuthin's matta . . ." Frank mouthed slowly,

drunkenly. His eyes were vague as he added something unintelligible.

Ralph Lowell picked up the ringing telephone and answered, "Rocky Ledge Lodge, good evening!"

"Hello, Ralph, this is Charlie over at Fieldstone. Say, did the two Hardy boys mention any change in plans?"

"Not that I know of, why?" Ralph responded.

"Well, it's nearly eight-thirty. They've got reservations here, but they haven't shown up."

"Hmm, I don't know what to tell you," Ralph said. "They left here right after breakfast. They seemed to be reliable fellows and experienced skiers—but there was a pretty rough blow late this afternoon. Maybe I'd better call Jack and have him get the search and rescue team ready."

"Okay, Ralph, and if they do come in, whenever it is, I'll call you."

As soon as Charlie hung up, Ralph dialed Jack Clayton. "I'll alert the crew," Jack assured him, "and we'll be ready to go at daylight."

Frank's condition was worsening by the minute. The violent shivering had stopped, but he was obviously disoriented. Joe realized that Frank didn't even recognize him.

"I've got to get you warm, that's what." Joe spoke in what he hoped was a reassuring manner. To himself he thought, "He's getting hypothermia! If I don't do something quick—" But Joe wouldn't allow that thought to continue.

"C'mere Frank," he said, putting an arm around his indifferent brother. "Sit here a moment." Grabbing two sticks, Joe moved the fire from against the rear cave wall out into the firepit he had dug. Then he returned to Frank.

"Here, old buddy, come in here." He reached for Frank's arm. Frank's head had sunk down onto his chest. "Frank!" Joe yelled, his voice cracking with fear, "Frank, wake up!" Frank's head raised slightly, but his eyes showed no recognition.

He would have to get Frank warmed quickly, Joe knew, remembering Professor Henry's warning that victims of hypothermia can die within two hours.

Joe crawled to Frank, took his arm and, pulling and pleading, got him into the deepest, warmest spot of the cave. Then, filling the steel cup from his survival kit with snow, Joe put it against the fire. He slid in beside Frank and opened both their down jackets. Putting his arms around Frank, Joe pulled Frank close to him, warming his brother with heat from his own body.

The snow in the cup melted, but Joe left it by the fire until the water was very hot. Then he emptied a packet of bouillon from his survival kit into the cup, stirred the broth, and forced Frank to drink it in order to warm him up from inside.

Frank seemed entirely removed from his surroundings and all that was happening. He had been muttering and mumbling, but that gave way to weak attempts to lie down.

Joe, however, would not let him lie down or sleep. Instead, he kept talking to Frank, asking him questions and answering them himself. He also insisted that Frank drink a second cup of the hot bouillon.

After what seemed an eternity, Frank finally responded to one of the questions.

"What?" Joe asked, and Frank repeated, "I said Harry drives a blue Chevy."

"Whew!" Joe breathed before he said as normally as he could, "Right you are. And how are you feeling?"

"I'm fine. Why?" Frank replied.

"Just wondered," Joe said casually. "What time is it anyway?"

"It's—hey, move over," Frank answered as he pulled his cuff back to look at his watch. "Wow! It's nearly ten o'clock. I had no idea it was so late." He looked at Joe in astonishment. "I must have dozed off. I lost track of time. Is it still snowing?"

"No," Joe said, "the wind and the snow stopped a while ago."

"Well, this is pretty cozy. I think we'd better stay put here until morning," Frank suggested, assuming his usual position of leadership. "It's too dark to ski safely and, besides, we've already missed dinner at the inn. Don't you agree?"

"That's fine with me," Joe answered, suddenly aware of a great but comfortable weariness. "As long as we keep the fire going we'll be fine—and we've got plenty of wood." He stole a relieved glance at Frank, who was staring into the fire thoughtfully.

"Did I doze off?" Frank asked. "I seem to have had some weird dreams, but they're hazy."

"Yes, you did," Joe answered. "But let's talk in the morning. We ought to get some sleep." He curled up, pillowing his head on his arm. "Just let's remember to keep the fire going."

Both boys fell asleep. From time to time one or the other would rouse as the flames burned low and the shallow cave became cool and add a few pieces of wood to the hot coals.

When daylight came they were delighted to see the clear blue sky overhead. They rose and gathered up their things, refolded the plastic and aluminum sheets and returned them to Joe's belt pouch.

"The survival kits sure passed the test, didn't they?" Frank commented with an easy smile.

"I wonder if you know just how well," Joe answered. "Do you remember much about last night—the early part?"

"Why, sure," Frank began, then added, "I remember you blowing the whistle to bring me in—" He hesitated. "And I sort of recall you making me drink something. But I don't remember clearly. . . ."

"There's a good reason why," Joe said quietly. "You had hypothermia."

"What! I can't believe it," Frank retorted. "Why, I know about hypothermia, and how to recognize the symptoms. . . ."

"Sure you do," Joe admitted, "but, as Professor Henry told us, the big danger with hypothermia is that an internally chilled body doesn't pump oxygen into the brain, and that means you can't make wise decisions for yourself." He looked at his brother.

"You began by shivering violently, then became disinterested in helping, which is unusual behavior for you. Then you were disoriented. Anyway, thanks to that survival course, you're fine now."

"Thanks to *you* I'm fine now," Frank corrected gently.

"What did you have to do to take care of me?"

"Exactly what Professor Henry recommended," Joe replied. He described his emergency treatment while they broke camp, putting out the fire until the ashes were cold.

"Well, little brother," Frank said slowly as they fastened their ski bindings, "I'm proud of you—and glad to have such a fine, competent partner!"

They were on the trail less than an hour when they met the search and rescue patrol coming from Fieldstone Inn.

"You boys were caught in the worst short storm we've had this year," Jack Clayton told them after he had radioed the second team, which was coming in from Rocky Ledge Lodge, to announce that the boys had been located.

"How'd you manage out in the cold all night?" one of the ski patrol asked.

"No problems at all," answered Joe quickly, winking at Frank.

"That's right," Frank said. "My brother here is a survival expert!"

Both boys laughed as they joined the search team on the four-mile run to a hearty breakfast at the inn.

The Six Stages of Hypothermia

1. Intense, uncontrollable shivering.
2. Violent shivering persists, speech becomes blurred.
3. Shivering gives way to loss of muscular coordination. Victim becomes disinterested in surroundings and the general situation.
4. Victim loses contact with his or her environment. Victim may become rigid. Pulse and respiration slow down.
5. Unconsciousness. Lack of response and loss of ability to function or respond to spoken word. Erratic heartbeat.
6. Heartbeat and breathing cease. Death follows shortly.

Ways to Combat Hypothermia

1. Share body warmth with victim.
2. Provide victim with hot liquids.
3. Use fire's warmth by directing fire's heat into shelter with reflector shield.

3.
Lonely Ordeal

"That shoulder strap seems to be bothering you," Joe commented as Frank tried repeatedly to make the buckle hold firmly in place.

"Yes," Frank replied, pushing the shock of dark hair off his forehead. "It keeps slipping. Let's stop early this evening so I can do a real repair job, all right?"

"Suits me." Joe grinned. "I'll go fishing while you work."

Their short lunch stop completed, the boys shouldered their backpacks and took off up the narrow, rocky trail.

Two days earlier Frank and Joe had left their car in a parking lot near the Adirondak Loj and began a planned six-day hike through the high peak area.

Frank wanted to add to his collection of wildflower photos. Joe, who cared little for picture taking, hoped to do battle with a record number of wild rainbow trout.

It was only three-thirty when they reached the lean-to in which they planned to spend the night, so there were more than two hours of daylight remaining. Quickly and efficiently the boys set up camp. They unrolled foam mats, placed them on the lean-to floor, and spread their sleeping bags on top.

While Joe gathered firewood, Frank refilled their canteens at a nearby spring. Then they put all their food supplies into Joe's pack and suspended it twelve feet above the ground on a rope strung between two tall birch trees.

"No racoon or bear can reach *that*," Joe said with satisfaction. He slid his small survival kit on his belt, then picked up his fly rod and tiny box of flies, and turned to Frank.

"According to the trail map that's in your pack, there's a small lake that way." He indicated the northwest edge of the high clearing in which the lean-to stood. "I'll just mosey down and catch us some fresh trout for supper."

Frank was busily engaged in dismantling the faulty strap from his packframe. He intended to replace it with one of the lashing straps that held his sleeping bag in place on the packframe.

"Huh?" he responded absentmindedly, not looking up from his task. "Okay. Good luck, see you later."

Joe disappeared from sight almost immediately as he left the clearing and dropped down into the steep-sided, heavily forested basin. He could not see the lake, but he had studied the topo map carefully during lunch, and knew it was right below the lean-to.

Crashing eagerly down the brush-covered slope, Joe was surprised how deep the basin was. By the time he reached the shore of the tiny, secluded pond it was four-thirty.

Not wanting to waste a moment of precious daylight, he immediately tied a #10 Cahill fly to his leader tippet and, flicking the rod experimentally a couple of times, he began casting.

Despite Joe's artful presentation, however, the trout didn't race one another to get to his lure. He slowly worked his way along the shore, occasionally changing flies, choosing different sizes and patterns as he patiently tried to get a fish to respond.

Suddenly there was a swirl as an eleven-inch rainbow lunged for Joe's line. When the trout felt the hook he leaped clear of the water, trying to shake free. Joe played the fish slowly and carefully, though, and was soon able to lift it onto the bank.

"You're a little beauty," he said admiringly, as he wrapped the fish in a damp fern-frond and tucked it into his shirt front.

He quickly caught three more smaller trout, all of which he released.

"I'll save you for next year," he promised each wriggling young fish as it swam away.

As the afternoon shadows lengthened, fishing action picked up and Joe became so engrossed he was unaware of the swift passage of time and of the threatening, overcast sky.

Approaching a weedy little cove, Joe tied on a Brown Wulff. He flicked the tiny lure lightly over the water. Wham! A large rainbow hit the fly even before it had settled on the mirrorlike surface of the pond. This one was a particularly big, strong fish. It took all of Joe's angling skill to bring the brawling, battling trout to land.

"Wait till Frank sees *this* one!" he exulted as he wrapped the big trout in a wet fern leaf. He put it inside his shirt front with the other fish. Then he snipped the soggy fly off his line, intending to replace it with a fresh, dry one.

"Boy, it's too dark now to see," he admitted to himself when he was unable to get the tip of his leader into the eye of the hook. "Guess I'd better quit fishing and get back to camp." He reeled in his line, took the rod apart, and looked about.

"Let's see now," he murmured. "Which way did I come down?"

He peered intently around the lakeshore. Nowhere was there a landmark to help him locate his starting point. He squinted up into the now dark forest but could not see the rim of the small, deep basin.

Joe closed his eyes to mentally visualize the topo map he'd studied. "All right, the lake was west-northwest of the lean-to," he recalled. "So I'll just head east-southeast—" He stopped. Which way was east-southeast? Why had he left his compass in his backpack? He looked up at the sky, trying to locate the Big Dipper in order to determine direction, but the overcast sky obliterated every star.

Frank, meanwhile, had repaired his shoulder strap satisfactorily. Also he had found a cluster of wild violets, a pair of graceful ladyslippers and a rock covered with lichen, all of which he had photographed in the warm afternoon sunlight.

Dusk was descending quickly and Frank began to prepare supper. He was becoming annoyed by Joe's lateness, although he well knew his brother's obsession with fishing.

Aiming his tiny flashlight at his watch, Frank saw that it was eight-thirty. No wonder he was so hungry! He put the coffee on and, as it came to a boil, he walked about the perimeter of the camp, calling out from time to time, "Joe! Hey, Joe! Where are you?"

Despite worry over his younger brother, Frank dished up

and ate his supper of freeze-dried spaghetti and meatballs.

"Where could he be?" Frank wondered, concern replacing his earlier annoyance. Reaching again for his flashlight, he unfolded the topo map and saw that there were four lakes in the vicinity of the lean-to. He also realized, as he studied the map, that he didn't know which lake Joe had gone to explore.

Frank washed his supper dishes and built up the fire so it would be visible enough to help his brother find his way back to camp in the dark. He then walked around again, calling Joe's name and blowing his whistle, but he got no response.

Eventually Frank slid into his sleeping bag. He slept very little, particularly after it started to rain. He knew it would be foolish to try and find Joe in the dark, but he spent the entire night tossing and turning and listening intently for any unusual sound.

Down on the lakeshore Joe lay crumpled and slightly dazed. When he realized he was lost he had forgotten his survival training—to stop, think, observe, and plan—and he had dashed around in a panic in the dark until he had stumbled and fallen.

The sound of his dropped fly rod clattering against the rocks brought Joe to his senses.

"Hey, boy," he said firmly, aloud. "Get a grip on yourself. All you've got to do is walk uphill, then circle the rim of the basin until you reach the lean-to."

He started to stand up, but a sharp pain in his right ankle forced him to sit down again—hard!

"Well, now you've done it," he muttered grimly, pulling up

his trouser leg. He immediately recognized the familiar, painful swelling as a sprain. Years before he had injured that ankle in a basketball game and it had been slightly weak ever since.

Joe realized then that he would have to spend the night where he was—away from camp, away from supper, and away from Frank who would, Joe knew, be upset by his absence.

"This is no big deal," he reassured himself. "I'll rig a little shelter, get a fire going, have a good fish dinner. . . ." But then a flood of guilt came over him. Frank would be up at the lean-to wondering and worrying about him—and it was all Joe's fault.

"I should have quit fishing sooner," he admitted. "Then none of this would have happened."

Slowly and cautiously Joe got up. Using a stout limb for a cane, he looked around for a good place to spend the night.

"Gotta get uphill a ways," he reasoned. "The bottom of this basin will be the coldest area." Spotting a small level shelf about twenty feet above the lakeshore, Joe limped upwards.

The shelf, he noted, had an abundance of good, dry firewood as well as several long, straight, strong limbs.

"First thing to do," he thought, "is to get a shelter built. Rain's due soon."

Reaching into his survival kit, Joe took out a coil of nylon parachute cord and a big plastic lawn bag.

"Okay, let's see, the wind will blow downhill tonight as the air cools; in the morning, when it warms up, the air will move back upwards." He looked about to select the location and direction of his shelter.

"I want the open edge parallel with the movement of any

wind," he mused, "to carry off the smoke from my fire. So I'll use those two trees for the main upright supports."

Joe picked up the longest, straightest limb he could find. Using two short lengths of cord, he lashed it parallel to the level ground of the small shelf, about three feet high, between a tree on the uphill side and a tree on the lower edge of the shelf. This bar would be the upper front ridge of his improvised lean-to.

Next he rolled a long, fallen log parallel to the upper bar, but about three feet behind the two upright trees. This would serve as the lower, ground-level edge of his shelter.

"Now for the covering," Joe said aloud, as he spread the big plastic lawn bag out flat. Using his pocketknife, he cut the bag down one side and across the bottom, which gave him a large sheet.

Gathering four marble-sized stones, Joe wrapped one in each corner of the plastic sheet. He then made rock grommets by tying each in place with about a foot of cord, leaving one long end of cord hanging loose. Using these four trailing ends, Joe lashed one edge of the plastic sheet to the upper bar and tied the lower edge to the log on the ground. This gave him a long, low, narrow lean-to roof.

Joe surveyed his handiwork with satisfaction. It would provide sufficient shelter for the night, even if it rained—and he knew it would rain.

"I'd better work fast," he urged himself as he began scraping a long, shallow firepit about four feet out from the open front edge of his lean-to. Next he fashioned a rough, rectangular

To make a rock grommet

1. Place small rock, piece of wood, or similar object near corner of
    plastic sheet.

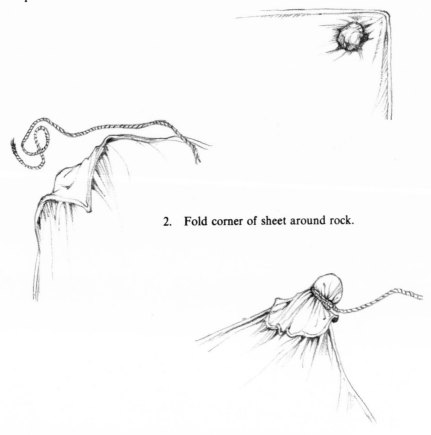

2. Fold corner of sheet around rock.

3. Tie cord tightly around rock. The same—or another, longer—
    cord can be used to secure sheet to lean-to frame.

frame of branches, which he covered with a sheet of aluminum foil from his survival kit. He propped this reflector screen be-

Aluminum reflector sheet positioned behind fire pit.

hind the firepit so it would push the heat into his shelter. Without a sleeping bag, he knew he would need the warmth.

"Ouch!" In his haste to get settled before the storm struck, he leaned a bit heavily on his sore ankle. In order to assure himself enough dry firewood to last throughout the night, Joe filled the back of his lean-to with small branches.

"Now that's downright cozy," he gloated as he looked about his snug Siwash* camp.

---

*Siwash. A rough, unplanned, poorly equipped emergency camp.

Soon he had a small fire blazing. The cleaned fish, wrapped in aluminum foil, were cooking in the coals. Joe considered the pros and cons of removing the boot from his aching foot. He finally decided just to loosen the laces. "Then I'll be able to tighten it up in the morning and get out of here."

After his supper of trout and cold mountain water, Joe stretched out to sleep. "As soon as daylight comes," he thought drowsily, "it will be easy to find my way back to camp."

Long before daybreak, Frank was up and dressed. Too worried to eat breakfast, he stuffed two small boxes of raisins in his pocket. Then he took out the topo map.

"Which lake did Joe say he wanted to try?" Frank asked himself. Each of the four basins was in a different direction from the lean-to. "If only I'd paid attention to him when he left!" Frank finally decided to head for the largest of the four lakes, which was in a northeasterly direction.

Before leaving camp, he wrote a note saying where he had gone and that he would be back after noon. He tied the note to his backpack, which he leaned against the shelter's rear wall.

At four o'clock, after a fruitless search, Frank returned, fully expecting his younger brother to be waiting for him. When Joe was not there, Frank decided to go for help.

"If I get started right away," he figured, "and hike until dark, I can make Moose Pond shelter tonight. Then I'll leave there early next morning and get to the lodge before noon."

Frank wrote a new note, explaining his plan, and transferred some food from Joe's to his own pack. Swinging the backpack onto his shoulders, he tightened the belt and set off briskly.

Earlier that same morning when Joe had awakened, he found his foot and ankle in worse condition than he had anticipated. It was badly swollen and very painful. Like Frank, Joe had a decision to make.

"There's no two ways about it," he reasoned. "I can't walk on this foot, especially up such a steep incline. I've really gotten myself into a mess, and I sure won't blame Frank if he gets mad at me," Joe admitted. "And I'd better start making some intelligent decisions. Okay, if the situation were reversed—if I were looking for Frank—how could he best help me?

"By staying *put*." Joe answered his own question. "Just as Professor Henry told us: 'Help rescuers find you by staying where you are and by making yourself as visible as possible.' "

Joe knew, too, that he must conserve his strength and energy for the long hike back to the car he and Frank had left parked near the Adirondak Loj.

"Actually," Joe conceded, "I'm in no serious trouble. After all, as Professor Henry said, 'A person can live for three minutes without air, for three days without water, and for three weeks without food.' "

Looking about with satisfaction, Joe assessed his situation. "I've got an almost full canteen, a pristine lake close at hand, nearly half a cooked trout, and a snug shelter." Firewood was plentiful and there were two packets of bouillon soup mix and some hard candies in his survival kit. "Under different circumstances," he thought, "I could enjoy this experience."

His throbbing ankle wouldn't support his weight, but Joe was sure the swelling would subside if he stayed off his feet. There was no need, either, to move about, except to fill his

THE HARDY BOYS HANDBOOK

canteen. Food gathering, he remembered from Professor Henry's survival course, was not recommended.

"Using up 2200 calories in order to gather food that offers only, say, 500 calories, is not a viable trade-off," was the way the professor had put it. "And, unless you're absolutely certain of what you are about to eat, you could poison yourself. Even if the poisoning is mild, it will make you feel ill and any vomiting will dehydrate you. So except in long-term survival situations, don't worry about lack of food. An empty stomach is preferable to one that is sick."

Joe settled down to wait as patiently as possible, sure that Frank would find him before long.

Frank reached the Adirondak Loj at noon on the fourth day after the boys had begun their hike. He described the situation to the manager, who immediately contacted the New York State Department of Conservation at nearby Ray Brook.

Within two hours eleven experienced mountaineers, all familiar with the area, were assembled at the lodge. The search team, comprised of trail maintenance crews, employees of both Adirondak and Johns Brook lodges, and "46-ers,"* was led by John Nichols of the Department of Conservation.

"Does your brother have a map and compass?" John asked.

"I believe he has his compass," Frank answered, "but I was carrying the map."

"Let's just hope Joe sits tight, wherever he is," John replied.

---

*A 46-er is a mountaineer who has scaled all forty-six peaks in the Adirondack high peak area.

"If he wanders around trying to get back to your camp he'll only make it harder for us to find him."

"There's a good chance he's hurt," Frank said quietly. "He's level-headed and woods-wise, so I doubt that he's lost."

"Well, we'll get started as soon as possible," John said as he spread a large-scale topographical map on the table. Everyone gathered around as he drew a grid of six squares around the lean-to from which Joe had disappeared.

"We can ignore that northeast sector," John said, "as well as the sector directly east-southeast of the lean-to. The areas we'll cover first are these four that contain the lakes." He indicated the four sectors with a blunt, calloused finger.

"I'll take team A, Bill will head up team B, Larry will take C, and Glenda will lead D team." John looked searchingly at Frank's grim, determined face, then added, "Suppose you go with the B team, Frank?"

"Fine," Frank agreed.

Each person then marked his or her own map with grid lines identical to those on John's map. The four teams were assigned to the four different sectors. Then, to save time, everyone climbed into John's pickup truck and they drove along a forest service road to get as close as possible to the search area.

Everyone had a backpack. In addition, each team leader carried a fairly elaborate first aid kit and a walkie-talkie. Each team member also wore a shiny, blaze-orange cap.

"I don't have an extra cap for you," John told Frank, "but since your backpack is safety-orange-colored, you'll be equally visible."

Looking the squad over, John said, "Okay, let's go. Good luck!"

Each three-person team took off at a smooth, mile-eating pace, heading for its assigned search territory. Frank's teammates, Bill and Tom, had the easy stride of the habitual hiker—deceptively slow as it covered the miles with remarkable speed.

Even though Frank had hiked nearly twelve miles that morning, his fine conditioning allowed him to keep up with the others with no discomfort. Just after dark they reached the lean-to where Joe's pack still hung, untouched.

"In the morning we'll reach our sector," Bill told Frank as they ate a quick, simple supper. Later, when Frank crawled into his sleeping bag, he slept soundly despite his continuing concern about Joe.

On the morning after his second night in the improvised camp, Joe sat watching a pair of ground squirrels playing hide-and-seek. Earlier he had held breathlessly still as three white-tailed deer ambled along, browsing unconcerned within twenty feet of his lean-to.

His enforced immobility, however, was becoming tedious. Except for hobbling around the immediate vicinity of his lean-to to gather firewood, plus one slow, careful trip to the pond for water, Joe had kept off his sprained ankle. He wanted it to heal sufficiently so he could climb up out of the basin. He was sure he could find the lean-to where he had left Frank, but he realized that getting there meant a lot of walking.

Bored, Joe leaned back against a tree trunk and idly scanned the high ridge beyond the basin's far upper edge. He noticed a tiny, bright-orange speck at the edge of a clearing. A moment later two more orange dots showed and all three moved slowly across the greenish-gray slope.

"Hey!" Joe yelled. He waved his arm but realized immediately the futility of trying to be seen or heard at such a distance.

With trembling fingers he grabbed his survival kit and pulled out his signal mirror.

"What's *that*?" Larry muttered, shielding his eyes from a brief, bright flash. He stopped and peered around. A moment later a similar, swift, blinding light swept across his face. This time he saw the source—something shining, flashing down near Deer Pond.

By then the other two C-team members had joined Larry on the clearing.

"One of you guys return that signal," Larry said as he flipped the switch on his walkie-talkie.

"Team C here," he announced. "Come in A or B—come in."

"You've got team B, Larry. Come back."

"We just received a mirror signal from Deer Pond," Larry replied. "And I think you fellows are closest. Will you check down there?"

"Sure thing. Will do," the scratchy voice answered. "Which side of the pond?"

"The east—repeat—*east* side." Larry spoke carefully. "We'll stay here to help guide you if necessary."

Bill, leader of team B, switched off his radio and blew two

short blasts on his whistle. At the shrill signal, Frank's tanned face went white. He stood immobilized for a moment, then broke into a run.

Less than an hour after he had signaled and received a return flash, Joe heard a voice faintly calling his name.

"I'm over here," he yelled. "Right over here!" Struggling, he pulled himself erect. Moments later a stocky, redheaded lad stepped into Joe's tiny camp.

"You must be Joe Hardy," he said, smiling.

"Yes," Joe replied, trying to hide his embarrassment with a grin and an outstretched hand. "Who are you?"

"I'm Bill Taylor," the young man answered, "and your brother Frank is right here with me." He looked around the neat camp, then turned back to Joe.

"Frank was right," he said. "You really *are* a good woodsman."

Just then Frank and Tom arrived, one coming in from the east, the other from the west.

"Hey, little brother!" Frank tried not to look too relieved. "Glad to see you." He looked down at Joe's swollen and discolored ankle. "Say, what happened?"

While Joe recounted his misadventure, Bill radioed the other teams to arrange a rendezvous at the lean-to above the basin. Then the boys set to work and disassembled Joe's camp.

Frank and Tom used a sturdy four-foot limb carried between them as a seat for Joe. Bill lashed Frank's and Tom's backpacks together so he could carry them while wearing his own. Then the quartet began the slow, arduous ascent, halting every fifty yards or so to rest or switch places.

The other teams were already at the lean-to when they arrived. The boys lowered Joe's backpack and divided the contents so the weight was evenly distributed. Frank then tied Joe's pack onto the back of his own.

Once on fairly level ground Joe was able, with the aid of an improvised crutch, to walk back to the pickup truck with only occasional assistance from the others.

"I sure am sorry to have spoiled our hike," Joe apologized as the Hardy boys drcve toward home next morning.

"You didn't *spoil* the trip." Frank grinned. "Your adventure added some unexpected drama. We met nice people and I learned good methods for conducting a search party."

"I guess you're right," Joe replied. "I must say, too, that the survival course sure was helpful!"

If you are stranded by yourself, your job is to:

- Overcome your feelings of guilt for inconveniencing others or of feeling incompetent. Take charge of the situation.
- Stay put. Particularly if you are injured, help rescuers find you by staying where you are and by making yourself as *visible* as possible.
- Build an emergency shelter.
- Provide heat. Prop a reflector screen (made from aluminum foil from the survival kit) behind your firepit to direct heat into your shelter.
- Make a decision between food gathering and conserving your energy. Except in long-term survival situations, don't worry about lack of food.

4.

Whitewater!

"I hope they haven't left without us!" Joe said as Frank pulled into the parking lot and cut the car's ignition. Although there were at least a dozen other cars parked there, River Rafting, Ltd. seemed to be deserted.

Frank and Joe, along with their friends Tony and Phil, went into the crude frame building that served as the outfitter's headquarters.

"Hi—anyone here?" Frank called.

"Howdy," a slender, tanned, blond youth smiled as he came through a rear doorway. "You the Hardy boys?"

"Yes," Joe answered, "and this is Tony Prito and Phil Cohen. We're sorry we're late. We were held up first by a flat tire and then, just a little while ago, by an overturned farm wagon. We helped the fellow get his chickens and peaches picked up, and there was just no place to call you from."

"Well, we've already sent the group out," the soft-voiced boy explained, "and we never like to take one raft alone—it's just not safe." He hesitated, looked at the four crestfallen faces, then added, "If you want to give it a try, though, we can probably catch up with them. But we'll have to hurry!"

"We'd really like to go," Frank answered as the others nodded eagerly.

"Okay, get your things together. I'll put one of the rafts on the truck."

The boys locked their wallets and watches in the car. Rabbit, as their guide introduced himself, produced a battered 50mm ammunition box. "Here," he said, "put your car keys, cameras and other stuff in here. This case is watertight. I'll tie it onto the raft."

Within an hour they had reached an access point on the Chatooga River, and launched the raft.* The five boys, each wearing a life vest and helmet, began an unforgettable downstream adventure.

"This ol' Chatooga," Rabbit told the boys, "makes a spectacular fifty-mile run through some exciting, wild country along the Georgia-South Carolina border."

"Wasn't the movie *Deliverance* made on this river?" Joe asked.

"Yep, it sure was," Rabbit answered. "And since then it's been made a National Wild and Scenic River. It's also become one of the most popular of all whitewater streams, at least in the eastern part of America."

Rabbit went on to explain that the Chatooga features enormous rock formations, broad, quiet stretches in which to relax and enjoy the mountain scenery, and also some exceptionally challenging rapids.

"We'll go through one particularly deep gorge," he prom-

---

*A sturdy eleven-foot long five-and-a-half-foot wide rubberized cloth raft.

ised, "where the cliffs rise more than four hundred feet above the water."

"Frank and I have rafted down the Colorado," Joe noted, "but this is really different. Out there they use huge rafts, operated by a professional oarsman. We were just passengers."

"These eleven-foot rafts are used on most of the eastern rivers," Rabbit responded. "We've found them best for our rivers. The riders enjoy paddling and generally they do very well. The guide on each raft paddles—and controls the steering—from the stern. . . ." His voice trailed off as he looked at his watch.

"The others got about an hour and a half headstart on us," he continued as the raft entered the river's fast flowing current. "But it's easy to see that you boys are all experienced paddlers. We'll catch up to them in no time."

"What a perfect day to be on the river!" Phil said, and he was right. It was a warm but clear, sparkling day with a cloudless blue sky overhead and specks of sunlight dancing on the water.

Frank straddled the raft's forward port side, with Joe behind him. Tony was seated across from Frank, on the starboard bow, and Phil was behind Tony. Rabbit sat squarely on the bulging stern.

The quintet swiftly slid into a smooth, effortless performance. When Rabbit called for a "Draw on the left" or a "Quick pry on the right" the boys, thanks to years of canoe paddling, responded immediately and effectively.

"What a beautiful river this is!" Tony commented as all four boys admired the steep, tree-clad banks and the curving, forward sweep of the swift waterway.

"Sure is," Rabbit agreed, "but it's treacherous, too. Claims a few victims every year—mostly fools who don't know what they're doing. Once in a while, though, it gets an experienced river runner."

As they approached each stretch of rapids, Rabbit explained the route he wanted to follow. "Soon as we pass that big boulder," he said, "we'll swing to the right, then straighten out and run into that V." With strength, stamina and skill at their command, the boys easily executed Rabbit's instruction.

"Let's pull over into that eddy a moment," he said, shortly after they had negotiated a fairly lengthy stretch of whitewater.

When the raft was out of the current, everyone squirmed around a little, flexing shoulder muscles, adjusting life-vest straps and helmets, and just relaxing a bit.

"Wanted to give you a little rest," Rabbit explained, " 'cause we've got a rough stretch ahead. It's a set of five waterfalls— chutes, we call them. There's a little slack water between each one, but they're close and we're going to be working hard until we're through the whole set."

The four boys had turned around and their eyes were riveted on Rabbit.

"You guys are good. We won't have any trouble. But I want you to be prepared and rested." His manner was still casual and easy, but there was no mistaking the serious undertone in his voice.

"The first is a little series of ledges, followed by a four-foot chute. We'll approach it straight on." He tightened his helmet strap. "Ready? Let's go!"

They dug their paddles into the water, swinging the raft back into the current and, always seeking the deepest channels, eased neatly down the ledges as though descending a flight of watery, uneven stairs. Then they dropped into the chute.

"Good work!" Rabbit yelled in order to be heard over the increasingly loud boom of tumbling whitewater.

"Now we have to hug the left bank to get into the next chute properly. Draw left! Now pull straight!" Again the boys negotiated the incredibly swift, churning current with seemingly effortless skill, which brought a broad grin of approval to Rabbit's smooth, tan face.

"This next one's really mean," he hollered. "It's a seven-foot drop with a terrific boil at the base."

The boys looked ahead to where the river entered a narrow channel between two big boulders. Then it disappeared out of sight as it plunged downstream. The roar of cascading water was deafening.

"We've got to approach from the right," Rabbit yelled. "I won't have time to tell you then, but the moment we hit the boil start back-paddling with all your strength. Here we go!"

From his seat astride the forward edge of the raft, Frank stared at the churning froth seven feet below. In preparation for the back stroke, he swung his paddle to the rear.

The very next moment he was struggling for his life!

With no warning whatsoever, Frank was snatched into the unbelievably powerful, deathly grip of the river. Like giant arms, its suction pulled him down.

"I have to get to the surface!" he realized, as he felt his lungs nearly bursting with the need for air.

A strong, capable swimmer with more than a little whitewater experience, Frank knew he was caught in a hydraulic. This occurs when water approaches the same point from two different directions. The resulting counteraction creates a tremendously powerful downward pressure.

The seven-foot waterfall they had entered cascaded against a huge, submerged boulder, which then thrust the water into a big standing wave. This reversed the direction of the river's flow and developed the hydraulic that trapped Frank.

He began to panic, frightened at being unable to breathe or to see anything but the dark green water surging about, clutching him in its inexorable grip.

"I'll never make it!" Frank was just about to accept his fate when his survival training took hold.

"S-T-O-P," he recalled. "Stop, Think, Observe and Plan." With that, renewed hope replaced his panic.

"Maybe I won't make it," he amended, "but I'll sure go down fighting!" He considered his options. He could continue struggling upward, or he could swim down deeper to get below the force of the hydraulic, then swim out from underneath and rise to the surface some distance away.

"If I'm to go down," he reasoned, "I'll have to remove this bouyant life vest." He reached for the top buckle, then stopped. "No, that's unwise. I'd better leave it on," he decided, and opted for one more last-ditch attempt to swim to the top.

Summoning all his remaining strength, Frank kicked his legs vigorously and forced his leaden arms to make a final, supreme effort.

Suddenly he was thrust free of the powerful, sucking hydraulic and felt, instead, the lightness of the surface water.

"Great!" he thought, "I've made it!" But at the same moment his head hit something, and he realized that he had come up underneath the raft!

There was, Frank knew, an air pocket of an inch or so under the raft's bottom. Pressing his face against the underside of the raft, he began to gulp air into his tortured, aching lungs.

Even though he was exhausted and hyperventilating,* Frank was able at last to breathe and evaluate his situation.

He was alive and safely out of the deadly hydraulic. But he was too fatigued and weakened by hyperventilating to be able to swim out from under the raft, which was plunging downstream toward still another waterfall.

And what of the others? Where was Joe, Phil, Tony and Rabbit? He was concerned about them all, but especially about his brother. Was Joe alive? Safe? Was anyone in position or condition to help *him*?

By now Frank was beginning to get his breathing under control. He was still too weary to get out from underneath the fast-moving raft, but he could think of ways to improve his situation.

"Maybe," he considered, "when I get to the next chute the raft will flip over, and I'll be able to swim free." Meanwhile, he clung to the raft's underside, his face still pressed against the bottom, into the air pocket. Although Frank was able to breathe, his legs bumped against the assorted rocks and boulders that lined the riverbed.

---

*Hyperventilating. Excessively rapid deep breathing. It results in a decrease of carbon dioxide in the blood, which can cause heart pounding, dizziness, numbness and increased anxiety.

Joe, who had been caught in the same hydraulic that had almost drowned Frank, was able to surface more easily than his brother. Having been thrown only into the edge of the fierce, sucking current, he came up quickly.

As soon as he surfaced downstream of the hydraulic, Joe looked around to see if his companions were safe. Tony, Phil and Rabbit were scattered along the western shore, standing or sitting in the shallow water near the bank.

"Hey!" he called, "Where's Frank?" Before anyone had time to respond, Joe realized that his brother might be trapped under the raft, which was now about thirty feet downstream.

Plunging immediately into the swift current, Joe quickly reached the raft. Grabbing one of its ropes, he reached underneath and felt Frank's hip.

"C'mere!" he yelled. "Frank's under the raft!" Rabbit dove into the water, intercepted the raft, and climbed aboard.

As soon as he felt someone on the raft, Frank began to signal. Clinging desperately to one of the raft's straps with one hand, he hit the underdeck in a series of hard, brisk, triple taps. Three, he knew, was the distress signal. He hoped that whoever was on the raft would recognize the difference between a bump against underwater obstacles and his signal.

Rabbit and Joe, however, were too busy to notice Frank's tapping.

"Hurry up!" Joe implored. "We're almost at the next waterfall!"

Rabbit jumped off the raft, but held tight to one of the side ropes. Joe, already in the water, locked arms with Rabbit. Thus anchored, he dove underneath and got hold of Frank's ankle. He tugged, trying to get his brother's attention.

At Joe's touch, Frank looked around, saw Joe and, releasing his white-knuckled grip on the strap, stretched his hand toward Joe. Together they paddled out into the sunlit water.

Both boys clung to the raft as Rabbit propelled it over to the shore. Tony and Phil, who had watched helplessly from the bank, ran down to help beach the water-filled raft.

Joe pulled himself from the river and went over to where Frank sat. Giving him a brotherly hug, he asked quietly, "You okay?"

"Yes," Frank answered, slowly and carefully, "I'm fine. But for a while there I must admit I was worried." He grinned weakly, then lay back, gazing gratefully at the clear blue sky overhead.

"Hey, will you look at that!" Rabbit spoke incredulously. "Frank's still hanging onto his paddle!"

Everyone, even Frank, glanced down. Sure enough, during the entire episode he had, like any experienced paddler, held tight to the tool he knew would be necessary to help him continue downstream.

When everyone had rested, the five boys emptied the raft of its accumulated river water. Then they relaunched it and climbed aboard to resume their journey to catch up with the main group.

Glancing back at Joe, Frank gave him a conspiratorial wink. "Well, I owe you another one, little brother," he said. "I'm sure glad you looked for me."

THE HARDY BOYS HANDBOOK

Tony, who overheard Frank, added, "Yes, Joe, you're the hero of the day." The others solemnly agreed, but Joe shook his head.

"No way!" he answered emphatically. "Frank is the real hero of this adventure. He kept his head when just about anyone would have panicked and done something stupid that could have killed him and maybe endangered others."

"Well," Frank responded, "if there's any credit to be given, it has to go to Professor Henry. In his survival course he impressed on us that no matter how desperately bad things may appear, you must remain calm and constantly try to improve your situation." He hesitated, then added, "It's not always easy—but it sure works!"

No matter how bad your situation appears

S-T-O-P

*S*top   *T*hink   *O*bserve   *P*lan

Survival training helps you

Fight panic
Think coolly
Make every effort to improve the situation
in order to save your own life

5.
Desperation in the Desert

"It sure handles beautifully!" Joe murmured appreciatively as he swung the sleek new bronze Wolverine back onto the highway.

"I'll say," Frank agreed. "I still prefer my little sports car, though I know Dad will be pleased with this one."

The boys were driving westward, delivering the new car Fenton Hardy had ordered two months earlier. The plans originally were for all three to pick up the car, then to drive into northern Michigan together for a fishing trip.

Mr. Hardy, formerly a New York police detective, had received an urgent request to assist the Phoenix police department with some undercover work. The trio therefore changed their plans. The two boys were to pick up the new car, drive it to Phoenix, meet their father there, then go to Lake Mead for the fishing trip.

"Sure wish I remembered to bring my tapes," Joe said when he was unable to find a radio station that played the modern jazz music he preferred. He fiddled with the dial a bit more, then switched off the radio.

"Yes," Frank replied, "and there are several other things we should have brought along—like my tool box and the survival kit."

"Oh, well," Joe answered. "It's no big deal—and we'll be in Phoenix by tomorrow. It'll be good to see Dad."

Frank nodded. "I'm looking forward to staying at that snazzy lodge while we fish. Usually we camp out and sometimes it's hard to face the cooking and cleaning after we've been hiking and fishing hard all day."

"Right!" Joe assented. "Walking into a lodge, taking a hot shower, and having dinner all cooked and served will be great. Still seems strange to be going on a fishing trip without any camping equipment."

Frank, who had been admiring the subtly colored southwestern desert, smiled in agreement, then changed the subject. "I bet there are some really interesting and beautiful views up on these side canyons," he mused.

"Well, we've been making terrific time," Joe responded. "We're at least a half day ahead of schedule and it's only ten o'clock. There's no reason why we can't make a short side trip. We might even find a few Indian cave drawings for you to photograph."

"Okay," Frank said with a grin. "Keep an eye out and we'll turn onto the next decent-looking road."

"There's one!" Joe announced fifteen minutes later. "See? On the left?" he gestured. "The sign says, TO BRUSHY BASIN."

Frank eased the car off the highway and onto the gravel road. As they slowed down for the turn, the car's engine stalled, but it started right up again when Frank twisted the ignition key.

"It did that yesterday, remember, when we stopped for gas?" Joe said.

"Probably just the heat," Frank commented as he eagerly looked ahead.

Soon the gravel road became a dirt one, but it was hard-packed and fairly smooth. Small canyons and rough arroyos led off on either side. Some had rutted jeep roads. Most were marked only by game trails.

Several times the boys stopped the car, got out and climbed up through the rugged, ridged desert country to one of the caves. None, however, showed any sign of Indian drawings, artifacts, or occupancy by creatures other than wildlife.

"Hey, there's a side canyon we can explore," Frank said. "Let's give it a try." Although it was obvious the road they turned onto was infrequently used, it had an even surface and, like the surrounding terrain, it was baked as hard as cement.

"Hold it! There's a rattler!" Joe pointed.

Frank hit the brakes, rolled down his window, grabbed his camera, and took several pictures of the coiled snake.

"He's at least three feet long," Frank said, "and with my telephoto lens, he'll look really impressive."

Like the first canyon they had explored, this one also had a network of side draws. When they saw one that appeared both interesting and navigable, the boys turned into it.

"I don't know about *you*, little brother," said Frank as they were returning to the car after looking into the cave, "but I'm ready for some refreshment!" He wiped the perspiration off his forehead with one finger. "Do we have any soda left in the little cooler?"

"I hope so!" Joe answered fervently. "Let's look." They opened the insulated box and found three cans, still slightly chilled, and four apples.

"We should have picked up more food and soda before we came in here," Joe said. "But of course, we never planned this."

"Why, this is a gourmet meal!" Frank joked as he looked around for a place to have their meager lunch. "Guess the other side of the car is the only shady spot," he suggested.

They sat down and started to eat. Frank bit into an apple, then took it from his lips, using it to point to the rim of the narrow canyon. "Look up there!" Silhouetted against the pale sky was a coyote. As the boys watched, a second and a third coyote came onto the rim, stood a moment, then moved out of sight. The first one stayed just a minute longer, then he too ran off the rim.

"Most people think of the desert as a *dead* place," Frank noted, "and it's just teeming with life."

Joe nodded. "Just today we've encountered a snake, lizards, eagles, prairie dogs, and now coyotes." He finished his soda and put the can in the cooler. "I'm sure there are deer, too, and a lot of other animals we haven't seen out here."

"Speaking of 'out here,'" Frank answered, "we'd better get back on the highway. It's nearly four-thirty."

They put the cooler in the trunk, climbed back into the car, and Frank turned the ignition switch. The engine rumbled and growled, but would not turn over. Frank tried again and again. Each time it was the same—grinding and grumbling, but no start.

"Sounds like it's flooded," Joe suggested.

Frank shrugged. "I can't see how, but we'll wait a few minutes, then try again."

A half hour later, after drawing on their combined mechanical knowledge, Frank and Joe were certain the problem was in the fuel pump.

"There's no way we can fix it," Frank stated flatly. "Even if I had my tool box, I doubt I could do much. The pump may be faulty and just needs to be replaced."

"Well, this is just great!" Joe moaned. "Here we are—miles from nowhere, no one knows we're here—and Dad's expecting us to have dinner with him in Phoenix tomorrow evening."

"Now, simmer down." Frank looked sternly at his younger brother. "We can't have come too far from the state highway. We'll just hike out and flag a passing motorist."

"Fine," Joe answered. "Just tell me one thing: which way is the highway?" He looked intently at his older brother. Frank stared back at Joe, then dropped his head.

"Good question," he admitted, sighing. "When we pulled off it we turned eastward, but we've been twisting and turning up and down through these canyons every which way. I have no idea where we are in relation to the highway. Of course, we can simply follow our tire tracks out, but there's one other problem—time. It'll be dark in about an hour."

The two boys sat quietly for several minutes, each contemplating their dilemma and considering ways to solve it.

"We've sure done everything wrong, haven't we?" Joe finally acknowledged, with a rueful shake of his head.

"What do you mean?" Frank asked.

"Well, first of all, we headed off into the boondocks without telling anyone our plans. Second, we came unprepared for any sort of emergency. Third, we paid no attention to where we went—you know, changing directions so often—and now we've gotten ourselves lost."

"You're right on every count," Frank agreed, staring thoughtfully through the windshield. The sun was low on the horizon, tinting the high buttes with an orange glow, while below the shadows lengthened and deepened.

"We'll have to stay here tonight and hike out by following our tire tracks in the morning," he added.

Once the sun set, the temperature dropped sharply. To keep warm, both boys put on sweaters. It was too crowded on either the front or rear seat for them to huddle together to share body warmth. Joe, the smaller of the two, curled up on the front seat while taller, huskier Frank squeezed into the back.

During the long, cold night, Frank was awakened by the sound of wind blowing sand against the car. Groggily he cranked the window shut and was soon sleeping again.

By morning the wind had stopped. The desert was clear, hot, and dry. The windstorm, however, had completely erased their tire tracks.

"If we knew which direction to take," Joe said, "we could chance hiking out, but we can't risk going the wrong way."

"Let's climb up on that high rim," Frank suggested. "Maybe we can see cars moving on the highway."

They scrambled up and scanned the entire horizon intently for more than two hours. However, they saw no sign of the highway or of any human activity.

"Looks like we're stuck," Frank said. "Remember Professor Henry's advice? 'Stay where you are—stay with your car.'"

"That's right," Joe admitted. "And we'd better follow that advice. I just hate, though, to sit here and do *nothing!*"

"Don't worry about that, little brother. We'll have *plenty* to do!" Joe raised his eyebrows questioningly as Frank continued, "No one knows we're here. Dad isn't expecting us to reach Phoenix before tonight. We have about half a canteen of water and, except for our fishing gear, we have no tools or equipment." He looked long and hard at Joe, then went on. "We may—and probably will—be here several days, so we'd better get busy preparing for it."

Joe nodded slowly, put his hands on his hips, grinned at Frank, and said, "All right, ol' buddy. According to survival's Rule of Three we can live three minutes without air, three days without water, and three weeks without food. Since we've got plenty of air, I guess our first and greatest concern is water."

"Correct! We've got to make a solar still. Do we have any plastic sheeting?"

Both boys thought for a moment, then Frank snapped his fingers. "Yes!" he answered himself. "Our dress suits are hanging in the cleaner's plastic bags."

"If there are two," Joe advised, "let's make two stills. One won't supply very much water."

Frank got the plastic bags and, using his fishing knife, slit them up one side and across the top. This gave him two sheets almost six by eight feet.

While he was preparing the bags, Joe removed a hubcap from one of the car's wheels and carried it twenty feet down the canyon. Using the hubcap as a scoop, he dug a hole three feet in diameter and two feet deep. Then he wiped the inside of the hubcap clean with his handkerchief and placed it like a bowl in the center of the hole.

"This one's ready," he called to Frank, who brought one of the plastic sheets to the freshly dug pit. They stretched it across

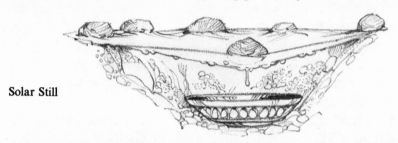

Solar Still

the opening and, using sand and rocks, anchored it in place. Then Frank placed a fist-sized rock right in the center of the plastic covering. This created a shallow, inverted cone with its point directly over the hubcap. As condensation formed underneath the plastic sheeting, it would drip into the "bowl."

"Let's move away a little to make the other still," Frank advised. "That way there'll be less competition for whatever moisture there is." Joe nodded, pulled off another hubcap, and soon the boys had a second solar still, up the canyon from the car.

"The sun is almost directly overhead now," Joe noted. "I don't know about you, but I'm getting hot and tired."

"So am I," Frank replied. "We'd better conserve what energy we have. The coolest, shadiest place is under the car. Let's get down there."

While the boys lay in the shade of the car they discussed their chances of being found, and considered various ways to help searchers locate them.

"Too bad that we're in a fairly deep canyon instead of out on the open flats," Frank said.

"That's true," Joe agreed. "And the tan car sure won't stand out."

"No. But we can make it more visible. Get your blaze-orange rain jacket. We'll tie it on the roof."

"Good idea!" Joe looked at Frank with open admiration. "We ought to think about signaling too. I'd hate to watch a plane go by and not make some attempt to let the pilot know we're here."

"Right. We should have a signal mirror handy." The Hardy boys looked at one another.

"Oh, no!" Joe almost whispered. "We *can't* pull the mirror off Dad's new car!"

"Oh, yes, we can," Frank answered firmly. "We'll do it as carefully as possible. But we must be able to signal, and you know a mirror is one of the best ways."

Joe rolled out from under the right side of the car while Frank pulled himself out on the opposite side. Together the boys examined the two side mirrors as well as the inside rearview mirror. None were attached with visible screws or bolts, but the one inside had an adjustable ball joint. Using the tip of his fishing-hook disgorger, Joe was able to disengage the mirror without too much damage.

"I'll lay it on the hood of the car," he said, "so if either of us hears a plane he can grab it and try to make contact."

"Fine. Let's tie that orange jacket in place," Frank said, "then get back under the car out of this heat." He opened the trunk, took the jacket out of Joe's duffel bag, then grabbed his tackle box. "We'll use fishing line to tie it down."

As soon as they had the bright-colored garment securely spread over the roof, the boys scuttled back into the relatively cool space under the car.

"Okay, you've mentioned the minus factors," Joe said when they were stretched out in the car's protective shade. "Now let's hear the pluses!" He turned toward Frank as he offered the challenge.

"Well, let's see . . ." Frank replied. "First we have a little water in the canteen. We also have two solar stills working. We have the car to shelter us from the hot sun during the day and to sleep in at night . . . ." His voice trailed off.

"It's after three o'clock," Joe said. "In a few hours Dad will begin looking for us. I sure hope he realizes we'd call if we expected to be too late to meet him for dinner."

"So do I. But right now I'm more concerned about a very dry throat. What do you say we drink what's in the canteen?"

"I'm thirsty too," Joe answered, "but shouldn't we ration what we have? Just take a couple of sips?"

"No. According to Professor Henry, you should drink what you need, if you have enough, and keep your body as moist as possible." Frank handed Joe the canteen. "There's not much in there, but take your share, then I'll finish it off. We won't be thirsty during the night, and by tomorrow we should have some water from those two stills."

As Mr. Hardy entered the Holiday Hotel in Phoenix he stopped at the desk.

"Have my sons arrived?" he asked the clerk.

"No, sir," the short, pudgy man answered, checking the register.

"Are there any messages for me?" Mr. Hardy requested.

Glancing at the mailboxes behind him, the clerk shook his head. "No."

"Thank you," the distinguished-looking detective replied, turning toward the elevators.

"That's odd," he thought. "It's nearly eight o'clock. Surely they'd call if they expected to be this late for dinner."

When he reached his room he removed his jacket and tie, hung them up, and sat down to read the evening newspaper. But he found himself unable to concentrate.

He was hungry but wanted to be near the phone in case Frank or Joe called. So he dialed room service and ordered his dinner sent up.

By ten-thirty he was convinced something had happened. Again he picked up the phone. He dialed the local police chief.

"I know you probably require a twenty-four hour absence to act on a missing persons report, Harry," he said, "but I know my boys, and I'm certain there's been an accident of some sort." He explained their planned route and meeting time. "Can you start the wheels turning?"

"Of course, Fenton," the chief answered. "We'll get on it right now. This is big country out here. They could've had a flat tire miles from nowhere, or maybe took a wrong turn. But don't you worry. We'll find your boys in no time."

"Thanks, Harry," Mr. Hardy replied. "I appreciate it. I'm at the Holiday. Call me as soon as you hear something."

"Will do, and don't worry."

"Wow, it's *cold* out here at night!" Joe said. "It's hard to believe it can be so hot all day then turn absolutely frosty when the sun goes down!"

The boys were in the car, wearing all the clothing they could put on. Neither of them had brought anything heavier than a light sweater since they were prepared for a warm weather vacation.

"We can make a heater," Frank suggested. "I think we're feeling the cold especially because we're hungry."

"If you mean to cut up the spare tire and burn the pieces in a hubcap—no!" Joe was aghast. "Good grief, Frank, Dad has never *seen* this car, and you're talking about tearing it apart!"

"I *was* thinking that," Frank admitted, "but maybe we can find enough scrub brush and thick sage branches so we won't have to chop up the spare. However, if we run out of other fuel, we'll make a stinky-stove. Remember, Joe, a tire is replaceable."

"All right, all right," Joe assented. "Let's see what we can scrounge." He climbed out of the car. There was not much light, but their eyes were accustomed to the darkness. Within twenty minutes the two boys had gathered a good-sized pile of gnarled, twisted wood. Frank pried off one of the two remaining hubcaps.

"Get a road map," he told Joe. "We'll use it for tinder."

Although neither boy smoked, they carried matches in their tackle boxes. Frank crumpled part of the map and placed it in the center of the inverted hubcap. Next he arranged the smallest, finest pieces of wood around the edge of the ball of paper.

"This heavy limb, plus the jack handle, will make a safe platform for the 'heater,' " Joe said as he placed those items on the car's rear floor.

"We'll have to keep the fire small," Frank announced. "And we ought to use a little oil to make sure the thicker wood burns thoroughly." He carried the hubcap to the front of the car. Joe raised the hood and, using the dipstick, dripped oil from the crankcase onto the wood in their improvised heater. Then Frank carried it back to the little platform Joe had made.

Heater Made With
Scrub Brush

He struck a match and, as the flame caught, the two boys exchanged a satisfied smile.

"Let there be warmth!" Joe said happily as he climbed back into the front seat and curled up for the night.

"Yes," Frank responded, "but we must keep a window cracked for ventilation." He piled extra firewood on the floor, then lay down on the rear seat. He folded his long legs as comfortably as he could, but his knees were up against his chest.

"It's warmer here right beside the fire than up front," he said. "So if you get cold, we'll switch places—okay?"

"I'm fine," Joe assured him. "And this way *you* have to tend the stove." He peeked over the seat and grinned. "G'night!"

Joe fell asleep almost immediately. His brother, however, lay staring at the small flame for quite a while as he thought about the predicament they had gotten themselves into. He was very hungry. They had had nothing to eat all day and no dinner the night before, just a scant cup of water apiece. How much water, he wondered, would their solar stills produce? And how much longer would he and Joe have to wait there until someone found them?

Mr. Hardy had finally drifted into an uneasy sleep. When the bedside phone rang it startled him.

"Hardy here," he answered, surprised to see daylight peeking along the edge of the drawn window blinds.

"Good morning, Fenton," the voice of Chief Robinson sounded hearty. "Your boys checked out of the Canyon Motel in Holbrook yesterday morning at eight-fifteen. They stopped for gas at Heber, which is about seventy miles east of Payson." He paused, then continued, "There's been no sign of them or the car since they left that gas station."

"If they left Holbrook yesterday morning, they were slightly ahead of schedule," Mr. Hardy replied slowly. "So they should have been here early. Have you checked alternate routes or side roads?"

"Yes—what few there are between here and Heber. As you know, that's just desert out there." He hesitated. "We're still looking. I just thought that it would be a good idea to report back to you."

"I appreciate it, Harry," Mr. Hardy told him. "The boys knew I'd be tied up until last evening. Maybe when they realized they had some extra time, they took a short side trip." He stopped a moment, then asked, "Is there any sort of attraction along the highway that would appeal to a couple of fellows— say an Indian village or a ghost town?"

"Not really, except maybe the old Zane Grey cabin. As I said, it's just rugged desert country. About the only people who go out there are rock hounds, hunters, and an occasional photographer."

"Is it necessary to have a four-wheel-drive vehicle to get into the desert?" Mr. Hardy queried.

"To get in very far, yes, but there are a few canyons with roads any car can make."

"Well, Harry, my guess is that Frank and Joe decided to take a closer look at the countryside. They may have gotten lost or stuck. Where can I hire a plane and pilot?"

"Our department of public safety has planes. We can make an air search. I'll also contact the sheriff's office and alert the Maricopa County Search & Rescue unit." He paused. "I'll get right on it. That desert can be rough, especially for anyone unused to the heat and lack of water."

"I'd like to accompany your pilot," Mr. Hardy said, "if that's possible."

"No problem at all. One of my men will pick you up in a half hour."

When he awoke in the morning, Joe was aware of being acutely uncomfortable. His mouth was so dry his tongue felt swollen. His eyes burned, his head ached, and his stomach was upset. He sat up, opened the car door so he could stretch out full length, then lay down again and went back to sleep.

Frank woke up when he heard the door open. Like Joe's, his mouth was dry, but he felt more hungry than thirsty. The fire in the hubcap heater was still burning, he noted, but the outside temperature was pleasant. It was that brief period between the nighttime's chill and daytime's dreadful heat.

Frank opened the other door and, using two sticks, carefully lifted the stove out onto the ground. He glanced at Joe and saw that he was still sleeping. Frank stretched to get the stiffness out of his legs. He knew he should conserve his energy but felt the need for exercise, so he decided to take a short, slow walk.

Although he was undeniably thirsty, he passed one of the stills without disturbing it. As soon as the plastic sheet was removed, all condensation would stop, and Frank wanted the still to generate as much water as possible. He also wanted Joe to be present when its production was revealed.

When Frank went back toward the car the sun's rays were

painting the striated cliffs with a ruddy orange glow. It was also getting hotter. As he ambled along, hoping his father realized he and Joe were in a jam, his eye caught an almost imperceptible motion about two yards to his left.

"A small desert rattler!" he realized, then looked about for a rock. He saw one nearby. Keeping his eyes on the snake, which was stretched to its full two-foot length, Frank eased slowly toward the softball-sized rock. He bent down cautiously, got a good grip on it, then turned toward the snake, which had not moved. Frank was within seven feet of the rattler when he brought his arm back, took aim, and threw with all his might. The snake died instantly, but Frank gave it another sharp blow on the head, just to be sure. Then, using a stick, he picked it up and carried it to the car.

"Hey, Joe!" he called as he approached. "We've got breakfast—wake up!"

Joe pulled himself up and stared at Frank for a long moment before his eyes shifted slowly to the snake. "That's nice," he muttered, "but to be honest, I'm really more interested in something to drink." His speech was slightly slurred, and Frank looked closely at his brother, whose lips were cracked and puffy.

"Sure thing!" Frank said, making a conscious effort to sound cheerful. "We'll break into one of the stills right away." Joe pulled himself out of the car and glanced at the hot walls of the canyon, then up at the sun. Then he dropped his head and covered his face with his hands.

"Come on, little brother," Frank said, throwing an arm

across Joe's shoulders. "Let's see what Mother Nature has for us." Joe let his hands drop, and smiled at Frank as well as his painfully swollen lips would allow.

Each boy took two corners of the plastic sheet and, very carefully, to avoid letting sand slide into the pit, pulled it away. Frank reached down and lifted the hubcap.

"Not quite enough for bathing," he said with a grin. "But there's nearly a cup and a half of water!" He handed the improvised catch basin to Joe. "Here you go." He smiled. "Better put your face down into it instead of trying to drink in the usual way. That rim isn't too clean."

Joe sucked the distilled water through his taut, hurting lips and into his parched throat.

"How does it taste?" Frank asked.

"Wonderful!" Joe sighed. "No—terrible, but wonderful, too." He took another sip, then handed the hubcap to Frank, who was laughing.

"That's a great description!" he said as he bent to take a drink. He held the water in his mouth a moment to taste it thoroughly. "My apologies, Joe," he amended, "your description was perfect. It's wet, and that's wonderful, but it'll never replace a cold mountain spring!"

Frank suggested they leave a little to drink after they cooked and ate the snake. Despite his nearly desperate thirst, Joe agreed.

While Frank cleaned and skinned the rattler, Joe built up the fire in their heater hubcap. Soon he had a good bed of red-hot coals ready.

"We'll use the dipstick as a rotisserie," Frank said. "But first

I'd better burn off the oil that's on it." He held the stick in the fire for a few minutes, then wiped it clean. Next he slid two-inch chunks of the firm, white snake meat onto the slender rod. Holding the meat above the coals, he turned it slowly until it was cooked through.

"You know, since we're short of water, we might eat some of this meat raw," he suggested. "That would give us more moisture than the cooked meat."

Joe grimaced. "Doesn't sound too appealing, but I'll give it a try. Let's cook most of it, though."

Despite the lack of seasoning, the fine-textured snake meat tasted mighty good to the hungry boys. "It's like rubbery crab meat," Joe commented thoughtfully.

Frank cooked all but a couple of pieces. "Here," he handed one to Joe, "chew on this, and squeeze all the juice out of it. I bet it'll help keep your mouth from drying out." Joe accepted the chunk of almost translucent meat, looked at it for a long moment, then resolutely popped it into his mouth.

"Now we'd better dig a third still," Frank told him. "We'll be emptying the second one this afternoon."

"We'll parallel Route 87 on the west side as we head north," Rick Atwood, the young police pilot, told Mr. Hardy as the little plane rose off the runway. "If we don't spot them, we'll move over and come back along the east side of the highway." He leveled off, checked his log sheet, then said, "They can't be too far off the road if they're in a regular passenger car. This area is four-wheel-drive country, so I expect we'll find them soon."

"I certainly hope so," Mr. Hardy responded. "I'm very glad you were available to help with this search."

"Do you hear something?" Frank asked. He and Joe were lying listlessly under the car.

"Huh?" Joe asked drowsily. He had been sleeping.

"Listen! I think it's a plane," Frank whispered. Both boys held breathlessly still until Joe said, "Yes! I hear it, too!" They rolled out into the afternoon sunshine and scrambled to their feet. Shading their eyes with their hands and turning slowly, they peered anxiously at the sky.

"I don't see a thing," Joe groaned, "But I *did* hear an engine—no question about that."

Frank continued looking, but finally he too conceded that there was no plane in sight.

"It's about time we broke into that other still," he suggested. Joe's lethargic depression worried him even more than his brother's flushed face and swollen, badly cracked lips. "You sit against the shady side of the car," he said. "I'll get the water."

Joe offered no resistance, but sat down as ordered. In a few moments Frank returned with the output of their second solar still. Its yield was almost the same as the other, a bit more than a cup and a half of water. Frank proffered the hubcap to his brother. Joe's hands trembled slightly as he accepted it and put his face down into the tepid water.

"Take a mouthful," Frank advised, "but don't swallow it right away. Hold it in your mouth for a minute first to get the most effect from the moisture."

Joe raised his face and nodded.

"Hey!" Frank yelled. "There's that sound again—only it's louder now—listen!"

Both boys looked up. Frank ran toward the front of the car and grabbed the mirror they had left on the hood.

"Might as well be ready!" he exclaimed.

"There's a lot of empty space out here," Mr. Hardy commented, "and so much of it looks the same."

"There is plenty of country," the pilot agreed, "but when you get familiar with it, every canyon and rim has its own characteristic that sets it apart."

The men were maintaining an alert watch, Rick Atwood out of the left window, and Mr. Hardy through the right side. They had flown northward as far as Payson and were now returning, heading back toward Phoenix along the eastern side of the highway.

As he rubbed his tiring eyes, Mr. Hardy felt the plane abruptly change its course. "See something?" he asked.

"Yeah, I thought I caught a glimpse of bright color—hunter's orange. We'll take a look."

"It *is* a plane!" Frank cried, as he put the mirror flat against his cheek, under his right eye. As soon as he saw the mirror's bright reflection of the sun on the ground in front of him, he extended his left arm and made an upright V with two fingers. Then he moved the mirror slowly until the bright spot was aimed through the base of the V.

Using the V like the front sight on a rifle, he aimed the mirror signal at the small plane that was passing them to the northwest. Frank did his best to hold the bright signal on the plane's front window. "He's turning! He's turning!" he shouted, continuing to beam his mirror at the plane.

Joe had come slowly to his feet and was watching the small plane approach.

"Wave at them!" Frank yelled. "Wave!" Joe waved and Frank, now that he knew they had been spotted, ceased signaling with the mirror and also waved. The plane's wings dipped. It moved away then returned, and the pilot again dipped his wings—a sure signal that the boys had been seen. Then the plane flew off.

Atwood immediately got on his radio. "We've found Mr.

Hardy's boys," he reported, then gave their location to the police dispatcher who responded to his message.

"It'll be dark in about an hour and a half," he told Mr. Hardy. "If the search and rescue team can't get them tonight, they'll surely be out early in the morning."

Mr. Hardy gripped the pilot's arm. "Thanks, Rick," was all he could say.

"It won't be long now." Frank placed his hands on his brother's shoulders. "We've got it made, Tiger!" Joe nodded and forced a painful smile.

Noting the setting sun, Frank adopted his take-charge tone. "It'll be dark and cold soon, so we'd better get ready for the night." He picked up the hubcap that had been in the solar still, took a mouthful of the stale, warm water, then passed it to Joe. "Finish it," he said, "while I get the heater ready."

Joe sucked the hubcap dry, then opened the car's front door and sat down, his feet on the desert floor.

Frank gathered more firewood, relighted the heater and set it on the floor of the back seat. By then it was almost dark.

"We may as well get some sleep," he suggested. "It'll be some time before a rescue party can get in here."

"All right," Joe agreed quietly and, turning on his side, he drew his knees up and closed his eyes. Frank shut the front door, then climbed into the back seat. He checked to be sure a window was open, then he too curled up and went to sleep.

When he awoke he could not see his watch, but he realized that the tiny heater was not keeping the car's interior warm enough for comfort.

"If *I'm* cold," he thought, "Joe must be colder." He sat up and looked at his brother. Joe appeared to be asleep, but he was also trembling.

Frank got out of the car, took the knife from his tackle box, and began cutting the cloth headliner from the car's ceiling. The decorative fabric, he noted, was backed with a foam noise-deadening material. "Good," Frank figured, "that will help make it warmer." He took the four-foot by seven-foot "blanket" and covered his brother. Then he moved the heater onto the floor up front. As he turned to climb into the back, he staggered.

"Guess I'm feeling the effects of the cold, thirst, and hunger," he reluctantly admitted to himself. He rested a moment, then crawled onto the back seat, curled up, and fell asleep while thinking, "I ought to go up onto that ridge and build a fire to help the searchers find us."

Frank never knew whether he was awakened by daylight shining on his face or the sound of a jeep's motor. He sat up, aware simultaneously of sound and light. His first conscious thought, though, was of Joe. He leaned over the front seat. Joe appeared to be sleeping peacefully.

"Hey, little brother!" Frank reached down and shook his shoulder. Joe stirred, started to stretch, then opened his eyes.

"Wassa matter?" he asked. "What're you doing?" As his eyes focused and he remembered where he was, he sighed deeply.

"Wake up, I hear a jeep," Frank said. "Sounds as if we're about to be rescued."

Joe sat up and managed a grin. "Really?" He listened. "Oh,

yes, I hear it too!" He leaned forward to open the door, looked down, then asked, "Hey, where did we get this blanket? Frank?"

But Frank was busy tapping the car's horn. It was a little weak but, after days of silence, sounded loud to the boys.

Within minutes, not one but two jeeps came up the canyon road. Mr. Hardy swung down out of the first vehicle, strode over, and hugged a son in each arm.

After allowing the family a brief reunion, the men from the search and rescue team came over and shook the boys' hands.

"You two fellows sure know how to take care of yourselves!" the slim leader of the group said with unconcealed admiration. "You've been out here since Monday night, haven't you? That's three days—a long stretch in this hot, dry desert country without equipment and supplies. How'd you manage?"

As they drove into town, the boys described their survival methods. Mr. Hardy, as Frank knew, approved of their use of the car's various parts.

"Mirrors, tires, hubcaps, and headliners can all be replaced," he said, "just as that faulty fuel pump must be. But you boys cannot. You did the right thing and I'm proud of you."

Travel Tips

- Always let others know your plans
- Carry emergency equipment and supplies
- Don't risk getting lost. Keep track of where you're going.

To cannibalize a car to survive, use

- A hubcap to dig with—and to catch the water from—a solar still
- A mirror for signaling
- The car for shelter
- The fabric headliner from the car ceiling to make a blanket
- A hubcap for a firepit, roadmaps for tinder, oil for starter fuel. Also burn chunks of tire to make an improvised heater (a stinky-stove)

Stinky-Stove Made With Tire Chunks

6.
The Unheard Flood Warning

Frank's knuckles were white as he fought to keep the car on the wet, winding mountain road.

"It's hard to see, isn't it?" Joe remarked.

"It sure is! This back road may be a good shortcut, but it's narrow and full of curves. And the wipers can't keep up with the rain," Frank said.

"This is some storm, all right," their friend Ralph Clark agreed from the back seat, "but we'll be at our house in about twenty minutes."

"It'll be good to get home," Ralph's twin, Harry, added. "That was a great spring vacation, but seven hours of sitting in the car is enough for me!" The four boys laughed.

"It's too bad your folks won't be there," Joe said. "Frank and I haven't seen them in a long while."

"They'll be sorry to miss you, too," Harry responded. "But you know they always go to Florida for the spring fishing. They'll be home Wednesday or Thursday."

"Hey!" Joe said. "I almost forgot! Here's a new album I want you fellows to hear." He slid a cartridge into the car's tape deck and the four boys listened appreciatively to the rhythmic beat of Joe's favorite band.

"Slow down, Frank," Ralph warned several minutes later. "The next turn to the left is our road."

"Okay," Frank replied. "Yours is the only house on this road, isn't it?"

"Yep. Our nearest neighbor, old Mrs. Knight, is a mile away," Ralph answered. "She lives along the river itself, while our house is on the north fork."

"There it is, ahead on the right." Harry leaned forward. "It's awfully dark, but I think you can see the driveway."

"Got it," Frank said, turning the wheel. "I don't know about the rest of you, but I'm ready to pile into bed right away."

"I think we all are," Ralph agreed. "Sit here a minute, though, until I turn on the porch light and unlock the door." He climbed out of the car and dashed through the rain. In a moment he stood in the lighted doorway, waving to the others to come on.

Grabbing suitcases from the trunk, the boys ran toward the shelter of the porch.

Joe exclaimed, "There must be three inches of water on the ground—look at my pants!" He pointed to the lower part of his jeans.

"We're all pretty wet," Harry concurred. "Let's get out of these clothes, have a cup of hot cocoa, and go to bed."

"Sounds good to me," Frank said, bending down to remove his shoes. "But let's not track up your mother's carpet."

Within a half hour the four boys were sleeping soundly, totally unaware of the warnings that had been broadcast throughout the area all during the day.

"Good work, men," Police Chief Babcock said as he looked at the weary faces of his small force of dedicated officers. "We've got everyone evacuated from the low areas—is that right?" Heads nodded in agreement. "And those up on the hill have been alerted, eh?" Again the men nodded.

Chief Babcock turned to his sturdy, gray-haired sergeant. "How fast is the river rising?"

"It's almost three feet higher than normal for springtime. River Road is already under seven inches of water," George Simpson answered. "And the rain is supposed to continue through tomorrow night. It looks bad."

"Charlie," the chief addressed the slender young man on his left, "you get roadblocks set up to keep people from coming into the valley. See that the barriers are manned around the clock. Only authorized personnel from the Red Cross, the state police, and medical or rescue squads are to come through."

"Yessir, Chief," the officer said. "I'll get on it right away."

"Hey, Joe—wake up!" Frank called sharply.

"Huh? What?" Joe rolled over and squinted across the room at his brother.

Frank, sitting up in his bed, appeared stunned. "Look!" he commanded, pointing at the floor. The urgency in his voice woke Joe completely. He leaned over and looked down.

"Good grief!" he gasped. "The whole room's flooded!"

"Shh," Frank said, "listen!" Above the steady pounding of heavy rain the boys heard an ominous low rumble. Frank rolled up his pajama pants and waded to the window.

"C'mere, Joe," he said, "you won't believe it."

Joe joined his brother and the Hardy boys stood together, staring silently at the scene outside.

Roiling, debris-filled water from the river's overflow rushed through the Clarks' yard. As they watched, wide-eyed, the powerful surge uprooted a budding young maple tree which, in turn, swept Mrs. Clark's garden cart out of sight.

"Look at the car," Joe whispered. "The water is halfway up the door!" Frank nodded in numb disbelief.

"We'd better wake Harry and Ralph," he said, turning away from the window. Joe followed him into the flooded hallway and up the stairs to the twins' adjoining rooms.

"What should we do?" Ralph asked after he and his brother had been awakened, told of the water on the first floor, and had viewed the devastation from their windows.

"Well, the first thing I'd suggest," Frank answered, "is to call the police and see what they recommend."

The four boys trooped into the hall and Harry picked up the phone, started to dial, then began tapping the operating buttons. He replaced the receiver. "It's dead," he stated grimly.

Joe stepped over to the wall and pushed the light switch. "No electricity, either," he announced quietly.

"That means we have no lights, no heat, and no cookstove," Ralph said in a flat, matter-of-fact tone.

"I think we'd better get out of here." Harry's usually deep, resonant voice sounded strained and tight.

"Not a bad idea," Frank agreed, "provided we *can*." He glanced at his companions. "First, though, let's get into some warm clothes. You fellows have boots, I know, but do you have any extras Joe and I can borrow?"

"Sure," Harry replied. "Our rubber hunting packs and hip boots are down in the basement." He and Ralph went into their rooms to get dressed as Frank and Joe returned to the guest room on the first floor.

"I'm glad we put our suitcases on these chairs!" Joe commented as he and Frank hurriedly pulled on jeans and sweatshirts. Sitting on their beds to keep out of the water on the floor, they rolled up their pant legs.

"Let's hope those boots fit us," Frank said as he stuffed clean socks into his shoes, tied the laces together, and hung them around his neck. Joe did the same.

The boys waded through the hall and into the kitchen just as Ralph and Harry came down from their upstairs rooms. Because of pressure from the water, Ralph was unable to open the door leading to the cellar unaided, so Frank helped him pull it ajar.

Ralph stood motionless, staring down the steps. "Oh no!" he said. "The basement's full of water!" He turned slowly to face the others. "*Now* what?"

"Let's see what it looks like outside," Joe suggested. The four boys waded to the back door.

"Wait!" Frank's voice was so stern and commanding that everyone halted. Frank moved forward and looked out through the door's upper, windowed section. "If we open this door," he warned, "we'll let even more water inside—it's at

91

least four feet deep out there." He scowled, shaking his head. "And that current is so swift it would wash us away!"

"Seems we're stuck here, fellows," Joe said, "so we'd better make the best of it."

Frank looked at his brother with approval. "Joe's right. The best place for us is upstairs, away from the water." Ralph and Harry looked stunned.

"Okay, let's get busy," Frank went on. "First we ought to gather up whatever groceries we can, and carry them upstairs. There's no telling how long we'll be here, so we may as well stay as well fed and comfortable as possible."

"I'll get stuff out of the fridge," Harry volunteered, relieved at having something to do. "There's no electricity so we should eat the perishable food first."

"What about cooking?" Ralph asked.

"Good question," Joe answered. "Do you still keep that charcoal grill in the pantry?" Ralph nodded. "We'll use that, then." Joe began to go for the grill and the bag of charcoal, but Ralph was already on the way.

Frank, meanwhile, had gathered up cooking pots, dishes, and tableware, and placed them in a large wicker basket. "We'll have to make several trips," he said. "Then, after we get the food upstairs, we ought to take other things like pictures, clothing, and furniture up there, too."

Nearly two hours later the four boys had gotten things set up for emergency living. They stored the family valuables in Mr. and Mrs. Clark's bedroom. The mattresses from the guestroom beds were on the floor of Harry's room. The charcoal grill, boxes of food, kitchen utensils, and cartons of cushions, clothing, and household linens were placed in Ralph's bedroom.

"Whew!" Ralph stood, hands on hips, and looked around his usually orderly room. In a moment his dismay gave way to a grin and he said, "Well now, how about some breakfast?"

"I thought you'd *never* offer!" Joe joked, and the four anxious but hungry boys laughed.

Harry poured some charcoal into the bowl of the portable grill. Before he lighted it, though, Frank opened one of the windows a few inches.

"Without ventilation," he explained, "that stove could quickly asphyxiate us."

As Ralph started to cook bacon and eggs, Joe measured instant coffee into cups. "Say," he mused, "I wonder if the water is safe to use?"

"I doubt that it's even *running*," Frank answered, "but if it is, we shouldn't risk drinking it without either boiling it for five minutes or using Clorox to purify it."

Joe carried the pot down the hall to the bathroom to see if the faucets would yield water. "Nope!" he announced when he returned. "The main is probably broken. I'll go get a bucketful from outside."

"Don't open the door," Frank reminded him. "Reach out through a window."

They were gathered around Ralph's desk, eating, when Harry suddenly jumped up. "I just thought—we don't have electricity, but I do have a little portable radio!" He dashed into his room, returning a moment later. "Let's try to find out what's going on." He pushed the button.

". . . have been safely evacuated from Milltown Valley, Chief Babcock said yesterday," the announcer's voice stated. "Evacuees are being housed in the gym at Hillside High School, where the Red Cross has set up cots and is serving soup and sandwiches to the nearly two hundred people forced to leave their homes. This is the worst flood ever to hit Milltown but, so far, no lives have been lost. Property damage, however, has already been estimated at nearly a million dollars." He paused. "After the following message from our sponsor I'll be back with the weather forecast."

"Everyone evacuated!" Joe repeated. "Ha! Obviously no one knows we're here."

"Heavy rain is expected to continue tonight," the announcer resumed, "but we can look for clearing skies by the following evening." Harry switched off the radio.

"Even after the rain stops, it'll take days before the water will recede enough so we can leave," Ralph commented.

"You're right," Frank agreed. "But as long as we keep warm and dry we'll be all right—provided we don't get sick or injured." He looked slowly from one boy to another.

"What we must do is sit tight, relax, and be careful," Frank continued. "We mustn't drink any water that isn't purified. We mustn't eat any food that might be spoiled. And we cannot act carelessly. A broken bone or a severe cut could be very troublesome, as well as painful." He smiled and added in a less serious tone, "This can't last very long— just a day or two, probably—and we have plenty of food and clothing, not to mention an *abundance* of water!"

"One problem though," Ralph interjected, "is that there's

not much charcoal left, and we're going to need the grill for heat as well as for cooking."

"How about firewood?" Joe asked after a moment of thoughtful silence. "Is there any stacked by the living room fireplace?"

"Of course!" Harry snapped his fingers. "I forgot about that. In fact, there's also wood by the fireplace in Dad's study." He took off his shoes and rolled up his trousers. "I'll go get it. The pieces on top will be dry, and we can dry out any that are wet."

"I'll help you," Joe offered, removing his shoes.

"Ralph, if you'll get some water, I'll wash these breakfast dishes," Frank volunteered, holding out a large pot. "Just scoop it off the floor downstairs," he added, "and bring up some detergent."

It was cold that night, so the boys carried Ralph's mattress and the grill into Harry's room. They closed the door and kept a small fire going all night, which was sufficient to heat the sealed-off but ventilated bedroom.

Next morning, while Frank stirred a pot of oatmeal bubbling on the stove, Ralph suddenly turned from the window and held both hands high.

"Listen!" he yelled, "I think I hear a chopper!" All four boys ran to the window, where they stood silently. The unmistakable whump, whump, whump of a helicopter got louder.

Frank raced into the master bedroom, and snatched the powerful flashlight he had noticed on Mr. Clark's bureau. He whirled, then threw open the window and leaned out.

He scanned the sky until he spotted the insect-like machine coming slowly up the valley. As soon as he saw it, he pushed the ON button and aimed the light beam toward the plane. When the tiny aircraft turned in his direction, Frank used one hand to cover the lens intermittently, and sent the DOT-DOT-DOT DASH-DASH-DASH DOT-DOT-DOT international distress signal.

"What a mess—the whole valley is completely flooded," the TV cameraman said as he photographed the ruin below.

"Yeah," the helicopter pilot answered, "I've never seen so much damage in such a small area." He shifted the big wad of gum in his mouth. "When's this film going to be broadcast?"

"It'll be on the eve—Hey! what's that?" The cameraman focused his lens on the upper part of a house nestled beside the north fork of the raging river. "Is that someone trying to signal us?"

The pilot looked, then swung the chopper toward the weak, flickering flash that had attracted his passenger and said, "Let's go see!"

"There are people in that house!" The cameraman zoomed in on three boys waving from an upper window. "I thought everyone had been evacuated from the valley."

"That's what I heard," the pilot responded as he switched his radio to SEND. "Wally," he spoke when someone responded. "Listen, call the rescue squad right away! There are some people trapped in a house up on the north fork road!"

"They saw us!" Harry's eyes were bright. "I saw the pilot wave!"

Less than two hours later the boys heard another sound.

This time it was the muffled roar of an outboard motor.

In a few minutes Craig Lamson, leader of the rescue squad, pulled his fourteen-foot boat up close to a ground floor window.

"We're sure glad to see you, Mr. Lamson!" Harry greeted him. "We'll be right down."

"It's a good thing you fellows signaled," Lamson commented as the four boys settled into the boat. "We thought everyone was safely out of here."

"Harry and I can't take any credit for thinking to signal," Ralph responded. "Frank and Joe Hardy here are the ones who took charge when we were stranded. They knew just what to do." He described how they had managed to cope with the problems they had faced.

Lamson looked appraisingly at Frank and Joe. "Well, you sure did everything right," he said, then turned back to Ralph. "And you picked good companions for such a rough adventure!" He smiled at all the boys, gunned his motor and headed for the Red Cross station.

Emergency Measures

If you are stranded in a house without heat, running water, cooking fuel, lights, etcetera, during an emergency, improvise with the equipment and supplies available.

Get yourself into the safest part of the house: a corner of the cellar in a tornado, earthquake or bombing; on an upper floor or the roof in a flood. Make a warm, cosy "nest" to stay in until the emergency is over or you are rescued. Gather food, clothing, medical supplies, et cetera, into the "nest" area.

Let others know where you are. Use signal devices, and keep a watch for potential rescuers.

7.
Jungle Plane Crash

"This weather is unbelievable. Just a few minutes ago the sunshine was almost blinding—and now *this*!" Frank's voice was slightly muffled by the small plane's engine.

Randy McNeil, pilot of the aircraft, had turned on the windshield wipers but they were of little aid. Slashing sheets of warm tropical rain erased everything outside the tiny charter plane's cabin. The view of the jungle-clad southern Andes below was completely obscured. They could barely see the propeller at the forward end of the fuselage.

Joe, who had been dozing in the rear seat, awoke and looked out. "Wow!" he said, "more rain. If you don't like the weather here, just wait a half hour and it will change." The trio laughed.

"We're across the high peaks," Randy told the boys. "We'll be landing at Valparaiso in about an hour and ten minutes, and you'll find the climate there on the coast more stable than here in the mountains."

"Dad said on the phone yesterday that it's been beautiful there," Joe responded. "Frank and I are looking forward to swimming with him on the beach at Vina del Mar. It'll be a real treat after working on that ranch near Cordoba!"

"It's exciting to fly through the rainstorm . . ." Frank began, when he noticed that McNeil was intently absorbed in his instrument panel, while at the same time he was fighting to control the plane's sudden erratic behavior.

"What's wrong?" Frank asked.

"My altimeter doesn't seem to be functioning," Randy answered. "And I'm having a hard time keeping the plane level. I wish I could at least *see*," he added uneasily.

Both Hardy boys sat quietly in order to allow McNeil to concentrate on the instrument panel dials and to regain full control of the craft.

Suddenly Joe broke the silence. "Hey!" he yelled. "Look!"

Despite the rain-caused obscurity, dense jungle foliage was clearly visible just below the wings. Randy struggled to pull the plane's nose up but, in spite of his efforts, the small craft ripped into the tree tops and, with a screeching jolt, lurched to a stop.

Frank's forehead bumped lightly against the windshield, while Joe's face bounced into the back of Frank's seat. Randy was thrown forward, jammed against the door. He appeared dazed. Frank reached across him and turned the ignition key to OFF.

The only sound then was the steady beating of rain against the fuselage.

"We'd better get out of here," Joe advised, "in case the plane explodes or catches fire."

"Right!" Frank concurred, then, turning to the pilot, "Are you okay, Randy?"

"Yes, I think so," McNeil muttered. But when he reached down to unfasten his seatbelt, he moaned in pain. "I must have bruised my left shoulder," he added. "It's probably not serious, but it sure hurts!"

Frank helped Randy release his seat belt, reached over and unlatched the pilot's door, then opened the door on his side of the cabin.

"Let's move as quickly as we can," he suggested, stepping out onto the right wing.

McNeil, cradling his left arm with his right hand, turned to climb out when Frank and Joe heard him gasp.

"What's wrong?" Joe asked.

"My knee," Randy replied. "I think it's broken!"

"Joe, come with me," Frank said as he crawled up over the top of the plane's cabin. He slid down onto the left wing, next to Randy's door. Joe followed, and the two boys helped the injured pilot out of his seat and onto the slightly tilted wing. The plane was tightly lodged in the thick foliage of the tree tops some twenty feet above the ground.

"We've got to get you to the ground," Frank told Randy. "Is there any rope in the plane?"

"There should be. There's a complete survival kit and a first aid kit, too, under the front seat." He spoke through clenched teeth.

Joe ducked back inside, pulled out the two metal boxes, and took a length of nylon rope from the one marked SURVIVAL.

"I know this will hurt," Frank warned the pilot sympathetically, "but we can't stay up here." As he spoke he tied one end of the strong rope around Randy's chest. "We'll be as gentle as possible."

"I'll go first," Joe suggested, "to clear branches and help Randy from below."

"Good," Frank agreed, "and I'll let him down to you." They were all anxious to escape from the potentially explosive aircraft as soon as possible.

With Joe leading the way and muscular Frank paying out the rope, Randy was carefully lowered to the ground. Frank pulled the rope back up and used it to tie the survival and first aid kits around his waist. Then he too climbed through the dripping, rain-drenched tree to the moss-covered ground below.

Together the boys helped Randy get away from the suspended plane. When they reached a small clearing about thirty yards north, they stopped.

With a sigh, Randy sank to the jungle's floor. "Thanks, fellows," he said, breathing heavily. "I don't know how I would have gotten down without your help."

Frank and Joe shrugged off his gratitude as Frank kneeled beside the suffering pilot. "Let's take a look at that leg," he demanded.

When McNeil exposed his knee, it was obvious to all three that the kneecap was badly smashed.

"We'll make a protective shield," Joe said, "to keep it from being hurt further, until we get you out of here."

Randy nodded wordlessly.

"And now, how about your shoulder?" Frank asked.

"It hurts—really hurts," McNeil answered softly, "even when I just move my hand."

Frank unbuttoned the pilot's shirt, then gently probed with his fingers. "Feels to me like it's dislocated," he said finally. "We'll do the same as for your knee—make a protective wrap, and try to keep you as comfortable as we can until help arrives."

"Shouldn't you make a splint?" Randy asked.

"No," Frank replied. "Neither Joe nor I can set bones properly, as a doctor can. We don't want to lock your knee or shoulder into what may be the wrong position, and have it set that way."

Randy nodded, accepting Frank's logic.

"Say, have you noticed the rain has stopped?" Joe asked.

Frank and Randy looked up, surprised. Neither had been aware of the weather change.

"Thank heavens for *that!*" Frank said, appreciatively. "Now we'd better take stock of things and get ourselves settled before the next shower." He brushed several insects away from his hot, moist face. "But let's take care of Randy first."

Joe opened the plane's first aid kit and removed rolls of gauze and adhesive tape and a tin of aspirin. Together he and Frank padded and bandaged the pilot's injured knee and shoulder. They gave him two aspirin, which he washed down with a cupped leaf full of fresh rain water.

"Here's some antiseptic salve," said Frank, handing a tube to Joe. "You'd better put some on that split lip."

Joe looked surprised, then gingerly touched his mouth. "I didn't even *feel* it," he said, spreading the soothing medication on his torn lip.

"What's in the survival kit?" he wondered, while he tried to open the second box. "Oh, great!" he exclaimed, "flares, as well as matches, a Space Blanket, signal mirror, and some mosquito netting."

"What's in that metal canister?" Frank asked.

Joe lifted the lid of the sealed tin. "Emergency food supplies," he announced, reading the label. "Hardtack, protein wafers, and Tropical Chocolate Bars."

"Oh, that's fine," Frank responded. "Now, let's get ourselves settled. If we don't reach Valparaiso they will send out searchers to look for us, though there's no way of knowing how long it will take to find us. So we'd better get comfortable." He looked over at McNeil. "How are you, Randy?"

"I'm okay," the plucky pilot replied. "But I'm sorry I can't help you fellows."

"Don't let that bother you," Frank assured him. "We just wish you weren't in such discomfort."

"This Space Blanket is too small to make a lean-to wide enough for all of us," Joe commented. "And, besides, we'll need it to keep Randy covered." He unfolded the reinforced aluminized sheet and carefully draped it over McNeil. "This will keep the moisture on the trees from dripping on you, and may help protect you from the pesky bugs."

"We have to build a shelter and start a fire," Frank warned. "If you'll gather firewood, Joe, I'll make us a hut that will offer better protection from rain than a lean-to."

While Joe cleared a firepit and began to stack all the dry wood he could find beside it, Frank constructed a large tripod. He lashed two sturdy ten-foot-long limbs to a third that measured nearly sixteen feet. He spread the ends apart, then tied several crosspieces horizontally from the shorter limbs to the long one, forming a rigid, triangular frame. Next he collected banana leaves from nearby trees until he had assembled a huge pile of the broad fronds.

After Joe had started the fire, Frank heated the leaves, which turned them from their bright, soft green, to a darker, glossier color. This made them more water repellent, as well as much more durable. Once the banana leaves were processed, Frank used them to thatch the hut frame, starting from the bottom and working upward to the pointed tip. Finally, using a stout stick, he dug a drainage ditch around the edge of their improvised shelter.

Because of the oppressive heat, both boys had removed their shirts. But they quickly put them back on because the moment their backs and chests were exposed hordes of buzzing, biting insects swarmed over them. Only when they stayed close to the fire did the Hardys find relief from the voracious bugs.

While Frank and Joe worked, Randy drifted into an uneasy sleep. Every time he moved, the pain of his injuries awakened him.

Frank drew Joe aside and whispered, "There's a small

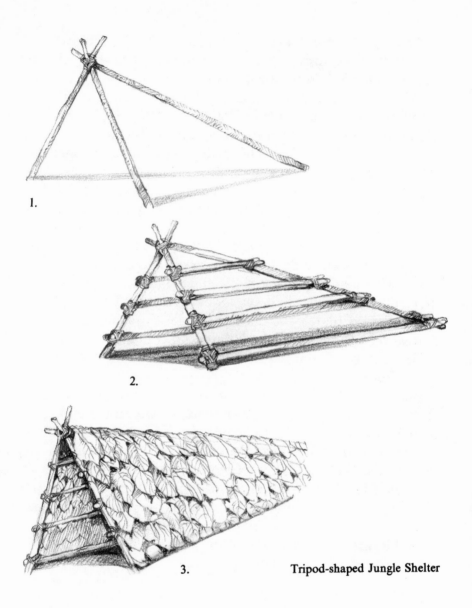

1.

2.

3. Tripod-shaped Jungle Shelter

bottle of stronger pain-killing pills in the first aid kit, but I think we should hold off giving them to him in case we're here more than a day or two. Randy will need them more later, I'm afraid."

Joe agreed. "Yes, he's napping now, but he could get worse, especially at night." He looked up at the sky. "It'll be dark soon, so I doubt that any search planes will be sent out before tomorrow morning."

Frank nodded. "I'm going to climb back up to the plane. If it was going to blow up or burn, it would have done it by now. And I want to try the radio—to give our location and describe Randy's injuries."

"Why don't you bring down some gasoline?" Joe asked as he swatted a mosquito. "If we get more rain, as I'm sure we will, it'll be hard to keep the fire going or to start a new one."

"Will do," Frank said, "and I'll grab anything else I think we can use." Before climbing up into the huge tree, he took the remaining length of nylon rope and tied it to his belt.

He returned about ten minutes later with a small bottle of gasoline and a duffel bag around his waist.

"Here's the gas," he said and handed the container to Joe. "I also brought dry clothes for us all, and some plastic cups I found. But both the radio and the plane's compass are broken." He wiped perspiration from his face and walked over to where Randy lay.

"I cleared away the branches, so the plane's bright red and white colors will be easy to spot," he told the pilot. "I'm sure we'll be found and out of here soon. Not tonight—it's too late—but probably by tomorrow."

McNeil looked up at Frank. "I hope so!" he said. "I filed our flight plan but, as you know, my instruments were not working properly just prior to the crash, so we could be somewhat off course." He shifted slightly, wincing with pain but biting his lip rather than crying out.

"I know you're hurting," Frank spoke softly and sympathetically, "but otherwise we're in good shape." He gestured toward the fire and the hut. "When you feel up to it, Joe and I will help you move over to the shelter, where you'll be more comfortable. We've got plenty of fresh water—the big banana tree leaves are full of rain water—and there are emergency food rations in the survival kit."

Joe came over to sit beside Randy. "In addition to those rations," he said, "there are bananas on the trees all around us, and a nice clear stream near by."

"I'll move whenever you can spare the time," Randy replied. "The bugs here are really bothersome." He glanced about apprehensively. "And I'm sure this place is full of snakes!"

"It's less buggy near the fire," Joe stated. "With us here snakes won't come into our camp area. We've also got mosquito netting to cover the hut's doorway. But before we put you inside, we have to build some beds to keep us off the damp ground and away from the crawling wildlife." He grinned encouragingly at Randy before he got up and began constructing raised beds out of bamboo poles for inside the shelter.

"While Joe's doing that," Frank said, "I'll get more firewood. We want to keep it going all night to discourage bugs and animals, and also to help searchers, just in case."

Although he maintained a brave front, it was evident to the Hardy boys that McNeil was suffering. He gritted his teeth to

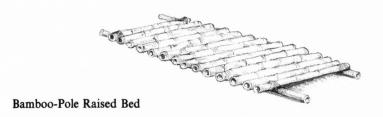

Bamboo-Pole Raised Bed

keep from complaining while they moved him onto the pallet in the hut.

During their supper of hardtack biscuits, protein wafers, bananas, and cocoa made from chocolate bars melted in hot water, Randy made a valiant effort to be cheerful.

The trio exchanged life stories and corny jokes until they all became sleepy. One by one, they dozed off.

"Oh-ooh-aaah!" the low groan woke Joe. He sat up and peered toward the sound. Light inside the hut was dim, just a flickering glow from the smoky fire outside.

"Randy?" Joe whispered. "You all right?"

"Oh, Joe, I'm all right," the pilot moaned, "just unbearably miserable. I don't know whether my knee or my shoulder hurts worse!"

Joe got up and went out to find the metal first aid chest.

111

Taking the vial of strong pain killers, he carried two capsules and a cup of water in to Randy.

"Here, fella," he said softly. "Take these."

"Thanks, Joe. I'm sorry I woke you." As McNeil eased back down, Joe heard the sharp intake of breath as another wave of pain swept through him.

"Don't worry about waking me," Joe answered. "I wish there was more I could do to relieve you. But those pain killers should help."

When Randy drifted off, Joe lay down and soon he too fell asleep.

In the morning the trio breakfasted around the fire on bananas, hardtack, and cocoa. Frank's well-built hut had kept them dry despite the night's intermittent rains.

"If there's no sign of a search plane today," Joe suggested, "maybe one of us should try walking out for help."

"Absolutely not!" replied Frank. "You know better than that, Joe. You know we should stay right here, together." As he spoke, Frank looked sternly at his brother and covertly cocked his head toward Randy.

The pilot, Joe noted, was unusually quiet and withdrawn. The pills had helped him sleep, and Frank had given him two more capsules before breakfast. Something more than the pain, Joe realized, was bothering him. "How are you doing, Randy?" he asked.

"Okay, thanks," McNeil answered. "And if you fellows want to walk out, I'll understand." His face was set resolutely. "This is a big chunk of jungle and there's a good chance we'll never

be found. I can't walk, but you might have to rescue yourselves. There's no point in all of us staying here to rot."

"Now *you're* talking nonsense," Frank retorted firmly. "You
know very well there will be searchers looking for us, and they
have a good idea where we are. You're in pain, we know, but
you'll be fine once a doctor sets those bones."

"Frank's right," Joe added. "I know you feel rotten but it's
very important to keep a positive attitude—that's one of the
major factors in being a successful survivor!"

Randy's eyes dropped in embarrassment, then he looked
back up at the boys.

"You two are something else!" He forced a self-conscious
smile. "I can't think of anyone I'd rather have crashed with!"
The three laughed together, breaking the tension.

"Now that that's settled," Frank announced, "we'd better
replenish our supply of firewood." Turning, he headed into the
forest.

No sooner had he disappeared, however, than Joe and Randy heard the distant sound of a plane coming steadily closer.
Frank noticed it too and rushed back to the tiny clearing. As
he raced to grab a flare from the survival kit, Randy cried, "It's
Will Vincent! I recognize his Cessna!"

At the same moment, the yellow and blue plane swept down
overhead, circled once, then disappeared. Joe shook the signal
mirror jubilantly. "He saw us, he saw us!" he shouted.

Less than two hours later a small helicopter arrived and lowered a rescue harness as it hovered over the makeshift camp.

Frank and Joe carefully placed Randy in the helicopter's

dangling webbed seat and strapped him in firmly.

"See you later." Randy managed a wavering smile as the copilot began winching him aloft.

"Sure thing!" The Hardy boys waved as the helicopter flew off. They knew that soon it would return for them.

Emergency Measures

- When you are in a crash, leave the vehicle immediately, but stay nearby to be easily seen from the air.
- Keep an injured person as comfortable as possible and move the person as little as possible. Encourage a positive attitude.
- Stay together. Make sure you are *visible*.
- Use survival kit and emergency supplies until you are rescued from the crash site.

8.
Rescue!

"Look there!" Joe pointed at the fresh footprints along the sandy river edge. "More bear tracks!"

Frank nodded absently and glanced at the early fall foliage before answering. "Well, this whole area is full of berries, so it's not surprising that there are lots of bears—they're feeding up against winter's hard times."

He shifted his backpack, then continued, "We have at least a couple more hours of daylight and, if we keep moving, we should be able to meet George right on schedule."

"That won't be hard," Joe replied. "Since we're carrying just two more days' food supply, the packs are nice and light. Let's grab a drink, then get going."

He dipped his metal cup into the cold, clear stream and offered it to Frank before refilling it for himself.

"This has been a good trip," Frank said. "I hate to see it end."

"So do I," Joe responded, "but it's not over yet. We still have a couple of days before we get to the south end of Lake Wenatchee." He slipped the cup's wire handle under his belt and the boys set off at a brisk pace down the narrow, overgrown trail.

Both Frank and Joe were tanned and fit after two weeks of strenuous hiking through the Wenatchee National Forest in northern Washington. Starting at Rainy Pass, they had followed the Pacific Crest Trail south as far as Glacier Peak. Soon after coming down from the peak, they left the trail and bushwacked east-southeast toward Lake Wenatchee, where they were to be picked up by a friend of their father's.

Shortly after leaving the narrow river, the boys came to a fork in the unmarked trail. Joe glanced at the sun, then swung to the right.

"Hold on a minute!" Frank called. "We'd better check this." He unzipped the little pocket on his shoulder strap and pulled out a topographical map and an orienteering compass. Using the tiny ruler at the end of the compass base, he measured the distance from where the trail left the stream to the fork where they stood.

"Take a look, Joe," he suggested. "According to this we should follow the more easterly route—see?"

Joe studied the map, then nodded in agreement. "You're right, ol' buddy." He refolded the map and handed it to Frank. "This is more fun than just walking along the main trail, isn't it?"

"Yes. Just so long as we keep a frequent check on our distances and direction." Frank winked at his brother, then pointed to the left fork. "Let's go!"

Ten minutes later they heard the sound of something crashing through the brush toward them.

"Watch it!" warned Frank. "That could be a bear!"

As the boys cautiously rounded a bend in the trail they came face to face with a thin, disheveled young man.

At sight of the Hardys the stranger stopped short. He took an unsteady step toward them, reached out a trembling hand and sank, sobbing, to the ground.

For a moment Frank and Joe just stared, then Frank bent down. "Hey, fella, what's the matter?"

"Is there something we can do?" Joe asked, kneeling beside the stranger.

"I think my friends are dying!" The words tumbled out as the young man struggled for self-control. "I decided to try and find a road—or a trail—to get help—"

"Where are your friends?" Frank demanded.

"Back that way," he gestured behind him, "by a lake."

"How far? And what's *wrong* that they may be dying?" Frank asked as he helped the nearly incoherent stranger to his feet.

"I don't know how far," he answered shakily. "I left them about an hour ago." He shuddered, lanky blond hair falling across his pale forehead. "But what's wrong is that they're starving, and just don't seem to *care*." He looked from Frank to Joe. "We thought we could live off the land, but there's nothing to *live off* around here!" His gaunt face flushed slightly. "We got lost, then ran out of food. We haven't had anything to eat in a couple of weeks."

While the young man was talking, Joe unbuckled his hip belt and slipped off his backpack. Reaching into a side pocket, he took out a plastic packet and handed it to the stranger.

"Here, you can munch on this trail snack while we go to the lake. It sounds as though your friends are in bad shape." He swung his pack onto his shoulders again. "What's your name?" he asked.

"Oh, I'm sorry—I'm Tom Adams," the young man introduced himself. "And thanks!" With trembling fingers he opened the little bag of dried fruit and nuts.

Frank and Joe followed Tom as he led the way, cramming food into his mouth as he walked.

"Eat slowly," Frank cautioned. "You might get cramps if you put too much into your stomach too quickly."

"I'll try," Tom mumbled as he chewed greedily. "But you just don't know how *good* this tastes!"

When the trail dipped down toward a small alpine lake, the Hardy boys saw a sagging tent set in a low, grassy clearing at the water's edge. Obviously it was the camp of inexperienced people, not knowledgeable woodsmen. The site was certain to be plagued by insects. The firepit, Frank and Joe noted, was placed upwind of the shabby, drooping tent, which was speckled with tiny burn holes from flying sparks.

"Where are your friends?" Joe asked.

"Probably in the tent," Tom answered as he walked toward the doorway. "Sam! Jim!" he cried. "Here are some people who can help us!" He held the flap open and the Hardy boys stepped inside.

Two wan, emaciated young fellows lay, fully clad, on their sleeping bags. As Frank and Joe knelt down and softly said "Hi there," both looked up weakly.

"That's Sam," Tom indicated the shorter, dark-haired boy. "And the redhead here is Jim."

"We're going to cook a meal for you," Frank told the silent, listless boys, "and you'll soon feel much better." He and Joe rose and went outside.

"Joe, you start a fire," Frank said as he began unpacking their remaining freeze-dried meals. "I'll get water and we'll feed these fellows."

Soon the Hardys carried cups and bowls of hot soup into the tent. Frank helped Jim sit up and eat while Joe assisted Sam. Tom was able to eat his portion of the nutritious chicken and vegetable broth unaided.

"Let that settle," Frank said, smiling, when they had finished, "and we'll have more solid food ready soon."

"Thanks—thanks a lot!" both Sam and Jim whispered gratefully, as they sank back on their beds. Tom, still clutching his empty soup bowl, followed the Hardys from the tent.

"You'll never know how glad I was to see you fellows," he said. "I didn't give up hope the way Sam and Jim did—and it was incredible finding you!" He eyed the bubbling pot suspended above the fire. "We really appreciate your helping us."

"We're glad we can," Frank replied, pouring a package marked "Spaghetti and Meatballs" into the pot. "I just wish we had more food. We're near the end of our trip, so we're down to the last of our supplies, but you're welcome to what we've got." He stirred the spaghetti. "How long have you three been out here?"

"We left Spokane on August twenty-eighth and hitchhiked

119

up to Chelan. Then we started walking into the wilderness. We had some—but not much—food with us because we wanted to try living off the land. We figured we'd find lots of wild things growing, and we planned to catch fish." He glanced ruefully at the boys, then continued, "None of us knows this country at all. Like I told you, we couldn't find anything growing that looked fit to eat, and the fishing has been terrible!"

"By the time we reached this spot we'd run out of food. We were weak and hungry and we were also lost . . ." He hung his head for a moment and sighed. "We sure made a mess of things."

"Not entirely," Joe consoled Tom. "Your friends gave up, but *you* didn't. All three of you were in a tough predicament—a real survival situation—but you never despaired, and that's the major factor in surviving. People who lose hope usually don't make it, while those who believe they'll live, do."

"As for living off the land, that's fine if you know how," Frank added. "But inexperienced people shouldn't try it." He took the pot off the fire. "This is ready. Let's have some dinner!" He, Tom, and Joe went back into the tent.

Sam and Jim already seemed somewhat revived, although they welcomed support as they tried to sit erect and eat.

"Take it slowly." Frank repeated the caution he had offered Tom earlier. "And chew thoroughly, or you might not be able to keep it down."

"This is the most delicious meal I've ever tasted!" Sam said. Frank and Joe laughed heartily.

"If you're okay now," Frank told them, "Joe and I will grab

a bite and set up our tent. We'll see that you get out of here safely just as soon as you're able."

After they finished the spaghetti, Joe offered to wash the dishes if Frank would put up their tent.

"Sure thing," Frank agreed. "But not right here! See that high spot?" He pointed to a level, raised promontory. "I'll put the tent there, where the breeze will keep the bugs away."

Next morning Joe cooked their last two packets of freeze-dried scrambled eggs and made a pot of coffee. Tom, Jim, and Sam were noticeably stronger and came out to sit around the fire where they ate with gusto, unaided.

"You fellows are making a fast recovery," Frank noted, "but it's a long, tough hike to the road. We'd better stay here at least one more day. Then, if you all feel strong enough, we'll head out."

"Have you guys got enough food to keep sharing with us?" Tom asked. "You said you didn't have much left."

"We've used it all," Joe admitted, "but there's food all around here we can gather."

"What?" The trio spoke in unison.

"Well," responded Frank, with a grin, "there are fish and berries and lichen and roots—lots more than you might think." He hesitated for a moment, then added, "If you want, Joe and I will show you some of the stuff that's available in what Joe calls Mother Nature's Supermarket."

"Boy, I'd sure like to see what there is to eat around here!" Tom spoke eagerly. "We couldn't find anything!" Jim and Sam nodded, wide-eyed, and Sam added, "Yes, please show us!"

"There's a way to catch fish that isn't sporting," Joe began, "but it's certainly acceptable when you need them for food."

"What way is that?" Jim asked.

"Net them," answered Joe. "And if you don't have a net, make one. I'll show you how." He took a cotton-net undershirt from his backpack. Spreading it flat, he tied a short piece of nylon cord around it, just below the sleeves. "A net shirt is best," he said, "but you can use almost any piece of clothing in an emergency." He stood up. "Sit tight, I'll be right back."

In a few minutes Joe returned with several slender saplings, each about six feet long. Taking one, he trimmed all the leaves off it with his knife. Then he wove the upper end of the flexible branch in and out of the lower edge of the net undershirt, bending the tip back to form an eighteen inch loop which he tied in place, leaving a three-foot handle.

"Now let's see if it works," Joe said, leading the way to the lake. He removed his boots and trousers, and waded slowly into the water. When he was several yards from shore he stopped and stood still for nearly five minutes, peering into the lake. Then with a swift, sure motion, he dipped the improvised net into the water.

"Got one!" He held the net aloft. A cutthroat trout wriggled inside. Joe waded ashore and placed the fish in the grass.

The three boys were stunned by his casual, expert success. They looked first at the glistening fish, then back at Joe with the awestruck expression of people who have witnessed a miracle.

"Wow!" breathed Jim. "If we'd only known that trick!"

"It's not a very big fish," Joe commented, "but there are plenty more in the lake. We'll have a good dinner tonight—especially if Frank gets us some vegetables and dessert to go with the fish."

Sam, Jim and Tom stared at Joe.

"Frank's going to gather some groceries," he explained. "Why don't you fellows go with him while I try to catch a few more trout?" The trio rose eagerly and turned toward Frank.

"Let's check around," he suggested, "and see what we can come up with." He handed each boy a cooking pot. "We'll use these to carry whatever we find." He started off briskly then, remembering the boys' weakened condition, slowed his stride.

Less than thirty yards from the campsite, Frank stopped. "Do any of you recognize this?" He indicated a small, prickly shrub. All three shook their heads.

"It's a wild rose bush," Frank said, "and these . . ."—he plucked the pods hanging on the slender stem—"are rose hips, which are very high in vitamin C." He opened several and

Rose Hips

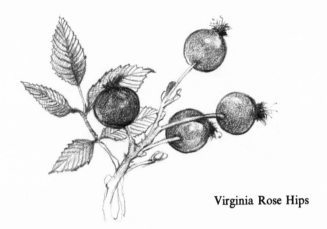

Virginia Rose Hips

passed them around for the boys to taste. Then they all gathered pods and put them in the small pot Sam carried. Soon they moved on.

"Surely you know that one," Frank said as he halted beside a huckleberry bush.

"They look like blueberries," Tom replied, "but we weren't sure, so we wouldn't take a chance."

"Well, that was wise," agreed Frank, "but I *am* sure, so let's

Blueberries

125

pick them." As they filled another of the pots, nibbling as they plucked the sweet berries, Frank suggested that the boys read some books on wild foods. "It's worthwhile to learn all you can about any area you plan to visit," he advised.

The group gathered salmonberries and some blackberries before Frank said, "These will be good to eat, but we should

Blackberries

look for other, more nutritious foods." He led them back toward the lake.

Salmonberries

"Ah," he cried, as they reached a slightly swampy area, "there are some marsh marigolds!" He bent to take the leaves and stems of the plants. "These are easy to identify by their star-shaped yellow flowers," he noted, "and will make a good

Marsh Marigolds

green vegetable to eat with Joe's fish." He then showed them

127

another plant nearby. "This is called miner's lettuce, even though you cook it. It's easy to recognize because of the way the stem appears to grow right through the leaves." Frank then recommended that they bring back some spruce needles for tea.

Miner's Lettuce

As they were gathering needles off nearby trees, he pointed up into the branches. "That bird's a blue grouse," he said, "and they're so easy to kill with a rock or even a stick, that they're sometimes called 'fool grouse.' If need be, we'll get one or two later, or tomorrow."

They walked a few steps farther when Frank suddenly knelt down. "Hey! Here's a real find!" Frank reached down to a short plant with crenated leaves, picked a leaf and, crushing it with his fingers, held his hand out to the group. "Smell this," he said, "and see if you recognize it." Jim was the first to respond.

"Ginger!" he spoke firmly. "Am I right?"

"You sure are," answered Frank, pulling up the roots of

Ginger

several plants. He peeled one with his knife, sliced it, and handed pieces to the boys. "You can eat ginger root raw or cook it. Either way, it's loaded with minerals and vitamins."

On their way back to camp, Frank also gathered some li-

chens, which, he explained, contain great food value. "But lichens," he warned, "should be cooked because they can make
you nauseous when eaten raw." The boys looked uneasily at
the reindeer moss and rock tripe in Frank's hand.

"We'll soak them overnight," he said, "and after they've
dried out, we'll powder them and make a jelly from the flour."
He laughed at the three serious faces. "Don't worry, it tastes
good when it's prepared, and is perfectly safe and very nutritious."

While Frank and the other boys were out gathering wild
foods, Joe had netted six more fish—three cutthroats and two
rainbow trout. He had also speared some frogs.

During the afternoon the Hardy boys discussed wilderness
survival with Sam, Jim, and Tom. "There are all sorts of wild
foods that are edible," Joe commented, "including the inner
bark of trees such as lodgepole pine and mountain ash. But the
most nutritious food by far is meat. A skillful hunter armed
with a rifle or shotgun is well equipped to feed himself. However, anyone can learn to capture animals, especially small
game, by setting snares." He pulled a coil of very fine wire
from his pocket. "A snare," he explained, "is just a slip noose,
set where it's likely to catch a critter like a rabbit or a squirrel.
You set rabbit snares along a rabbit trail, for example, with a
loop about four inches across, suspending it an inch or so
above the ground." Seeing that he had the undivided attention
of the trio, Joe continued. "Squirrels are particularly easy to
catch. You can set several snares—smaller, of course, than
those for rabbits—along one pole. You lean the pole against a

Rabbit or Squirrel Snare

conifer, and you may capture several squirrels in a day." He turned to his brother. "Anything you want to add?"

"Well," Frank replied, "I'd suggest frogs as an easy-to-catch food source. You can spear them, as Joe did, or just grab them with your hands. Skin them, clean out the insides, and roast them over the coals." He pointed toward the lakeshore. "As you can see, there are plenty of frogs all around.

"Another animal that has saved the lives of so many people stranded in the wilderness is the porcupine." Frank grinned at the looks of surprise. "Porky is so slow-moving he can be killed by a blow with a stick. Just be absolutely sure he's dead before you attempt to skin and clean him! The meat, by the way, is very good—something like pork—and very nutritious because of its fat content." Frank stood up and stretched. "I think we ought to quit *talking* about food, and get busy preparing supper—what do you say?"

"Yay!" the group chorused.

The Hardys, assisted by the swiftly recovering boys, cooked up a hearty, tasty meal of trout, frogs, miner's lettuce and marsh marigolds (which they boiled like spinach). Ginger root, and spruce tea added extra flavor, and for dessert they ate rose hips and assorted berries.

"Wow, this is good!" Sam sounded so surprised everyone burst into loud laughter.

"Now I know why Joe calls it Mother Nature's Supermarket," Tom added. "Everything we need is out here, if we just learn to 'shop' for it."

"We'll gather more food tomorrow," Frank said, "then begin our trek to the highway, picking and catching what we need along the way. You all seem to be in good enough condition to hike, if we don't try to cover too much ground too fast."

"Sure," Jim replied, "I think we're able to get underway— eh, fellows?"

"Yep, sure," Sam and Tom agreed.

Next morning they broke camp. Frank and Joe added the boys' heavier equipment to their own packs, so the recuperating trio would not have burdens they were unable to manage. Even so, it took three instead of two days to reach the spot where George Lichtenberg was to meet them.

He was there, sitting in his car, when the group arrived.

Frank introduced Tom, Sam and Jim, and told his father's friend that he and Joe had promised them a ride back to Spokane.

"Sure thing!" George assured them, a warm smile creasing his smooth, pudgy face. "When you and Joe weren't here two days ago I figured you'd be along soon, so I left a note in the trail register over there" he pointed, "and came back each afternoon." He helped the boys stow the packs in the trunk, then added, "I didn't worry about you, though I would have in another day or so. Now I want to hear about your hike!"

"While we drive these fellows to Spokane," Joe promised, "we'll give you the whole story." The group crowded into the car and George Lichtenberg swung it onto the road.

"We left the Pacific Crest Trail just east of Glacier Peak . . ." Frank began to describe their adventure modestly. But the trio he and Joe had rescued frequently interrupted in order to give George a clear picture of the Hardys' expertise.

After leaving their new friends at Jim's home, George turned approvingly to the Hardys. "I'm proud of you both," he told them. "Taking that survival course was wise—especially because you were able to use your skill and knowledge to help those boys."

"You can say that again!" Frank and Joe replied in unison.

Don't attempt to do something beyond your own abilities.

- Eat only those wild foods you recognize as safe.
- Take no chances with plants that might be toxic.
- Purify all questionable drinking water.
- When fuel is at a premium, keep heated area small.
- Above all, think POSITIVELY to assure survival.

Glossary

Alloy. A combination of two or more metals, sometimes with other substances added.

Alpine. Pertaining to elevation of the high mountains.

Aluminum foil. In the survival kit to make a reflector-sheet behind fire, to use as an improvised cup, to wrap and cook food in, or to shape into a drinking straw or funnel.

Arroyo. A small, steep-sided, flat-bottomed gulch created by fast-flowing water, but usually dry. Found chiefly in the southwest.

Asphyxiate. To suffocate.

Aspirin. A mild pain-killer available in the survival kit for relieving toothache, headache, or discomfort from an injury.

Band-Aids. In the survival kit for covering cuts or abrasions, or to patch down garments until a permanent repair can be made.

Bandanna. In the survival kit to use as a scarf, a hat (tie knots in each corner), a sling for an injured arm, a bandage, or a towel.

Boulder. A large, rounded rock.

Bouillon packets. In the survival kit to make a tasty, nutritious, hot drink when dissolved in a cup of hot water.

Bushwack. Making one's way across trail-less or unmarked country.

Candle. In the survival kit to use for light, to 'move' fire from one site to another, to use as a lubricant on balky zippers, to use for temporary mending (drip hot wax over small rips in down clothing), or to waterproof boots.

Canyon. A deep, steep-sided valley.

Charms candy. In the survival kit to provide quick energy. Since Charms are made with glucose instead of white sugar, they will *ease* instead of *increase* thirst.

Chute. A steep, narrow descent, such as a short waterfall.

Clorox. To purify water, two drops of Clorox per pint of water can be used if water purification tablets are not available.

Conifer. A cone-bearing evergreen tree or shrub.

Crenated leaves. Leaves with a scalloped edge.

Cutthroat trout. A handsome trout found in the western states. It has a rosy stripe similar to a rainbow trout, as well as black speckles, but its outstanding characteristic is the bright red slash at its throat.

Dot-Dot-Dot Dash-Dash-Dash Dot-Dot-Dot. The international distress signal.

Fishing-hook disgorger. A tool somewhat like long-handed pliers, used to reach into a fish's mouth to disengage an embedded hook.

Fuselage. The body of an airplane, to which the wings, tail structure, and engine are attached.

Ginger root. The dark yellow or light reddish-brown root of the reedlike ginger plant.

Grouse. A gamebird similar to domestic fowl. There are several species of grouse native to North America.

Hardtack. A hard, saltless biscuit used instead of bread during long trips, such as on shipboard.

Herringbone. A pattern consisting of vertical rows of V's. Used in skiing to walk uphill.

Huckleberry. Another name for blueberry (sometimes called whortleberry).

Hydraulic. A canoeing term for powerful downward pressure caused by water approaching the same point from two directions.

Hyperventilation. Excessively rapid deep breathing which results in a decrease of carbon dioxide in the blood.

Hypothermia. Severe reduction of bodycore temperature.

Insect repellent. In the survival kit to prevent annoying and potentially dangerous insect stings.

Lichens. A nutritious fungus that grows in leafy, crusty, or branching forms on rocks and trees.

Lip balm. In the survival kit to protect lips from sunburn or chapping. Can also be rubbed onto hands or face for similar protection.

Lodgepole pine. This tree and others such as mountain ash, poplars, etcetra, have an edible inner bark underneath the outer bark, and offer some nourishment. The bark can be eaten raw, dried in the sun and chewed, or cooked.

Marsh marigolds. Small plant found along streams and swamps with a star-shaped yellow flower. The leaves and stems are very tasty when cooked.

Metal Match. An implement in the survival kit used to draw sharply against the blade of a steel knife in order to strike sparks—for sure-fire-starting.

Miner's lettuce. This salad plant is easy to recognize because the stem seems to grow *through* the leaves. Leaves and stems may be eaten raw or boiled as a hot vegetable.

Multivitamins. In the survival kit to help stave off malnutrition and to keep up strength and energy when food is scarce or nonexistent.

Nylon parachute cord. Available in the survival kit to lash limbs together to build a lean-to, to tie plastic sheeting to a lean-to frame, or to lash the framework of a fire reflector.

Orienteering compass. A compass set in a ¼-inch thick sheet of clear lucite, 2 to 3 inches wide, 3 to 6 inches long, marked as a ruler. The compass housing turns a full 360 degrees.

This type is the easiest compass to use in plotting a course on a map.

Panic. Sudden overwhelming fear that often results in hysterical behavior.

Plastic lawn bag. In the survival kit for shelter. Either wear it, use it to cover a lean-to frame, or use it as the cover for a solar still.

Plastic whistle. In the survival kit to save one's voice while trying to get the attention of rescuers.

Protective shield. Thick, heavy wrappings of cloth. Extra-heavy protective bandages.

Protein wafers. Thin, hard cookies with a high protein content, available in mountaineering shops and health food stores.

Rainbow trout. Feisty fish that thrive virtually wherever there is clean, cool water. Liberally spotted with black specks, the distinguishing feature is a broad band of color that ranges from pale pink to bright red, depending upon the water in which it is found. The band runs all along the fish's side.

Raised beds. Platforms made of wood or other materials built to keep the sleeper off wet, insect- or snake-infested ground.

Reindeer moss. Gray, branched lichens that grow in arctic and subarctic regions, a favorite food of reindeer and caribou.

Rock grommet. Used in shelter-building, a rock tucked and tied in the corner of a sheet. The rock serves as a fastener to tie the sheet in place.

Rock tripe. Thin, irregular-shaped lichen. Gray, brown or black, the small "discs" attach themselves to rocks by means of a short stem.

Rose hips. This red-orange fruit that grows wild on rose bushes is very high in vitamin C.

Salmonberry. A raspberry-like fruit found in the northwest. It is named for its color.

Schuss. Skiing swiftly downhill without slowing speed.

Sierra Club cup. In the survival kit to drink from, heat water in, and use as a tiny cooking pot. Also, used as a catch-basin in a solar still.

Signal mirror. In the survival kit to signal potential rescuers. A well-aimed beam from a good glass mirror will carry a bright sun signal for up to fifteen miles.

Single-edge razor blade.   In the survival kit to use as a knife in case you haven't brought a belt or pocket knife.

Siwash camp.   A rough, poorly equipped, unplanned camp.

Snares.   A slip knot tied in very thin, pliable wire, and set in a place where small animals such as squirrels, rabbits, and even birds may be trapped when they step on the trigger holding the snare in place.

Solar still.   A makeshift device to use the sun's heat to distill water condensed from the ground.

Space Blanket.   Aluminized sheet made with reinforced fiberglass threads, 5-by-8 feet, red or blue on one side, silver on the other. Used to construct a shelter to wrap oneself in or to use as a signaling device (when laid on the ground).

Spruce needles.   Needles from a spruce tree. Boil a few in water for a tea that's rich in vitamin C.

Steel wool.   In the survival kit to use as waterproof tinder, into which sparks from a Metal Match are aimed.

Stinky-stove.   A heater made from an inverted hubcap, filled with cut-up tire chunks or kindling, over which crankcase oil is dripped to make the fire burn well.

Tinder. Highly flammable material which will catch fire easily from a spark.

Topographical maps. Maps prepared by the U.S. Geological Survey, which show elevation from sea level, type of vegetation, water, and contour of terrain.

Tropical Chocolate Bars. Made by Hershey, they are smaller and harder than regular chocolate bars. They will not melt in hot weather.

Water purification tablets. All questionable water must be made safe before drinking. Boiling water for five minutes is an accepted purification method, but some water will be lost in steam. These tablets (or Clorox) purify the water while retaining every drop, which is necessary when water is scarce.

Whitewater. Roiling, frothy water found in rapids—the opposite of flat water, which is smooth and tranquil.

Wire saw. Included in the survival kit for cutting limbs to proper length for a lean-to, reflector frame, or crutch.